D1106950

THE FRANKLIN LIBRARY
OF MYSTERY MASTERPIECES

THE D.A. CALLS IT MURDER

The name Erle Stanley Gardner has been almost synonymous with Perry Mason since Gardner began writing about the brilliant defense attorney in 1933. For more than three decades, he churned out yarn after suspenseful yarn about the unstoppable Mason, and the enormous success of the Mason stories made him one of America's most popular authors—and one of the richest mystery writers of all time.

Mason was only one of Gardner's many serial characters, and he was not the first. The author had written volumes of short stories about such characters as "Phantom Crook" Ed Jenkins, confidence man Lester Lieth, and Speed Dash, the "human fly," long before he penned a Mason case. Even after the success of the Mason series, Gardner was not content to write only about one character. He needed to balance his writing, to find an alter-ego for Mason's unfailing defense attorney. He found what he needed in 1937 when he created Doug Selby, the unbeatable district attorney of Madison County, California.

Selby starred in nine novels, beginning with *The D.A. Calls It Murder*. Although he resembles Mason in many respects—he is young, handsome, single, and righteous— Selby sits at the prosecutor's table, and that makes all the difference. Whereas Mason defends his client, Selby defends the entire community, and he does so tirelessly, despite the fact that his constituents frequently doubt his abilities and question his theories.

The D.A. Calls It Murder traces Selby's investigation into the mysterious death of a clergyman at the Madison Hotel.

Although the signs point to suicide, Selby suspects foul play. His search for the truth leads him from Madison County to Hollywood and introduces him to a cast of unusual and mysterious characters that includes a glamorous starlet, a secretive hotel manager, and a muckraking reporter bent on destroying the D.A.'s career.

Born in 1889, Erle Stanley Gardner spent his childhood traveling throughout California, Oregon, and Alaska with his father, a mining engineer. As a teenager he promoted unlicensed boxing matches; later, he went to college but was promptly kicked out for punching a professor. In 1909 he took a job as a typist in a law office. After reading law on his own, he passed the California bar in 1911.

Although Gardner loved the law, he found he couldn't make much money defending the type of clients he chose (usually penniless Chinese and Mexican laborers), and so in 1921 he began writing fiction. He sold his first story to a pulp magazine in 1923, and from then on writing became his passion. He would work at the law all day, then write all night, averaging about 4,000 words before going to bed in the early morning hours.

Erle Stanley Gardner died in 1970, leaving behind more than 100 novels, countless short stories, and several works of non-fiction. His most important legacy, however, was his influence on the courtroom melodrama. Gardner's fiction defined the form, and years after his death, both the form and his fiction endure.

The Editors

THE D.A.

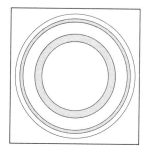

CALLS IT
MURDER

Erle Stanley
Gardner

THE FRANKLIN LIBRARY
FRANKLIN CENTER, PENNSYLVANIA

This is a Franklin Mystery published by The Franklin Library.

The frontispiece by David Tamura was specially
commissioned by The Franklin Library for this edition.

Copyright 1937 by Erle Stanley Gardner. Renewed 1964 by Jean
Bethell Gardner and Grace Naso. Published by arrangement
with William Morrow & Company, Inc.

Special contents copyright © 1989 The Franklin Library.

The acid-free paper used in this book conforms with the standards
for permanence and durability set by the Council of Library
Resources and the American National Standards Institute.

Printed in the United States of America.

For information about other Franklin Library programs,
write to The Franklin Library, Franklin Center, PA 19091.
The Franklin Mint is a quality manufacturer of
specialty collector's items.

❖   ❖   ❖   ❖   ❖   ❖   ❖   ❖   ❖   ❖   ❖   ❖

THE D.A. CALLS IT MURDER

1

The room held a subtle atmosphere of burnt-out activity. Physically, it had the littered appearance of a vacant lot from which a carnival had moved away. The walls were decorated with posters. "ELECT DOUGLAS SELBY DISTRICT ATTORNEY" screamed one poster. Above the words appeared the likeness of a handsome young man with curly hair, a devil-may-care glint in his penetrating eyes, and a forceful, although shapely, mouth. Hanging beside it, a twin poster showed a man some twenty-five years older, wearing a big sombrero, his leathery face creased into a friendly smile. It required a close inspection to show the hard determination of the gray eyes. That poster bore the words: "VOTE FOR REX BRANDON FOR SHERIFF."

Half a dozen small desks and tables had been crowded into the room. They were littered with envelopes, pamphlets, windshield stickers, and other campaign paraphernalia.

Douglas Selby, newly elected district attorney, grinned

3

across the room at Sheriff Brandon. It had been a bitterly contested battle, involving an election contest, a re-count of ballots, and an action in mandamus. The actual election had been history for weeks, but the political backers of the two men had kept the room in the Madison Hotel for post-election activities.

Selby, crossing his long legs, ran his hand through his thick shock of curly hair and said, "Well, Rex, in fifteen minutes we start for the courthouse to take charge. Personally, now that it's all over, I'm going to miss the fight of the campaign."

Rex Brandon fished a cloth sack from his pocket, shook flakes of tobacco into a brown cigarette paper. His thick fingers rolled the cigarette with an expert twist. He moistened the edge of the paper with his tongue, stroked the cigarette into a smooth cylinder and said, "You'll have plenty of fighting, son. It ain't all over—not by a long ways."

Selby, at ease, was as relaxed as a cat sprawled in the sunlight. "Not much they can do once we get in office," he drawled.

Sheriff Brandon snapped a match into flame with a quick flip of his thumbnail. "Listen, Doug, I'm twenty-five years older than you are. I haven't got as much book learnin' but I know men. I'm proud of this county. I was born and raised here. I've seen it change from horse and buggy to automobile and tractor. I remember when you'd never walk down the street without stopping three or four times in a block to pass the time of day with friends. Now things are different. Everyone's in a hurry."

The sheriff paused to apply the match to the end of his cigarette.

"What's that got to do with us?" Selby asked.

"Just this, son: People used to know pretty much what was going on in the county and office holders used to get a square deal. Now people are too busy and too selfish to care. They've got too many worries of their own to bother very much about seeing that other people get a square deal.

"If it was just politics, it wouldn't be so bad. But during the last four years the doors have been opened to all the scum from the big cities. Chaps who haven't been big enough to work a racket in the Big-Time have drifted in with a lot of little, vicious, chiseling, crooked stuff. Sam Roper, the old district attorney, either got a cut or should have had one. You know that as well as I do.

"Now, then, it's up to you and me to clean up this mess."

"It's already cleaned up," Selby pointed out. "The crooks read their death sentences in the election returns. They've been getting out. Little hole-in-the-wall joints have closed up, or turned honest."

"Some of 'em have, and some of 'em haven't," Brandon said. "But the main thing is that *we've* got to watch our step, particularly at the start. If we make just one major mistake, they'll hoot us out of office."

Selby looked at his watch, got to his feet and said grimly, "It's going to take a hell of a lot of hooting to get *me* out of office. Come on, Rex, let's go."

Campaign headquarters had been located on the top floor of the Madison Hotel. As the two men stepped through the door into the carpeted hotel corridor, a door opened midway down the hallway on the right-hand side. An apologetic little man, attired in a black frock coat and wearing a ministerial collar, slipped out into the hallway. He seemed to be tiptoeing as he walked rapidly toward the elevator and pressed the button.

It was several seconds before the elevator cage rumbled up to the top floor, and Douglas Selby studied the little minister as they waited. He was between forty-five and fifty-five, and fully a head shorter than the district attorney. The small-boned frame seemed almost fragile beneath the shiny cloth of the well-worn frock coat.

As the elevator operator opened the sliding door, the little clergyman stepped into the cage and said, in the precise tones of one accustomed to making announcements from a pulpit, "The *third* floor. Let me off at the *third* floor, please."

Selby and the sheriff entered the elevator. Over the top of the minister's unsuspecting head, Rex Brandon gave the tall young district attorney a solemn wink. When the elevator had discharged its passenger at the third floor, the sheriff grinned and said, "Bet there's more funerals than weddings where he comes from."

The district attorney, immersed in thoughtful silence, didn't answer until they were half way across the hotel lobby. Then he said, "If I were going to indulge in a little deductive reasoning, I'd say his parish was controlled by one very wealthy and very selfish individual. That minister's learned to walk softly so as not to offend some selfish big shot."

"Or maybe he's that way because his wife has a natural talent for debate," the sheriff grinned. "But, say, buddy, don't forget that this speculating business ain't just a game. Did it ever occur to you that during the next four years whenever a crime's committed in this county it's going to be up to us to solve it?"

Selby took the sheriff's arm and headed toward the white marble courthouse.

"You solve the crimes, Sheriff," he said, grinning. "*I* simply prosecute the criminals you arrest."

"You go to the devil, Doug Selby," the sheriff rumbled.

2

Douglas Selby had been in office just twenty-four hours. He surveyed the littered material on his desk, reached a decision and summoned his three deputies.

"Boys," Selby said, "I'm tackling a job I don't know much about. You boys have got to carry most of the load.

"You play ball with me and I'll play ball with you. Gordon, it's up to you to instruct these boys in the duties of the office. Among you, you've got to handle the routine.

"Here's a bunch of stuff which has piled up on my desk. There's everything here from a complaint about a neighbor's dog scratching up a front lawn to a tip that someone is selling liquor without a license. You boys take this stuff into the law library and divide it up. Don't write any more letters than you have to—telephone people, get them to come in, reason with them, straighten things out by diplomacy. Don't fight unless you have to. When you once start to fight, never back down. Remember that *The Clarion* will give us a square deal and *The Blade* will be fighting us all the way. You'll make mistakes, but don't let the fear of making mistakes keep you from reaching decisions. Whatever happens, don't let anyone bluff you. Whenever you . . ."

The telephone rang. Selby said, "Just a minute. . . . Hello."

Rex Brandon's voice, sounding rather strained, said, "Doug, drop whatever you're doing and come down to the Madison Hotel right away. They've found a dead man in one of the rooms."

"What is it," Selby asked, "murder, suicide or natural death?"

"They don't know. They say it's a minister. . . . I have an idea it's the same chap who rode down in the elevator with us yesterday."

"Where are you now?" Selby asked.

"I'm at the City Hall, picking up the chief of police. We'll get to the hotel a few minutes before you do. The room number is three twenty-one. Go right on up. We'll meet there."

Selby said, "Okay, Rex," hung up the telephone receiver and turned to his deputies. "You boys go to it," he instructed. "You'll have to handle the routine business of the office."

Grabbing his hat, Selby raced down the marble corridor of the courthouse, took the steps of the wide staircase two at a time, jumped into his car and drove to the Madison Hotel.

He noticed that Brandon was ahead of him. The sheriff's car, equipped with red spotlight and siren, was parked in the red "no parking" zone in front of the hotel. Moreover, a portion of the street was closed off where a force of men were installing one of the new ornamental lighting fixtures the city had recently purchased. Selby found himself caught in a traffic jam and it took him nearly ten minutes to extricate himself, find a parking place for his car and return to the hotel.

George Cushing, owner of the hotel, and the one to whom Selby had been indebted for the room used as campaign headquarters, approached with smiling affability.

A man in his early fifties, Cushing tried to maintain an air of smart, urban sophistication. He wore a pin-striped blue serge suit, meticulously pressed, and cut for men twenty years his junior. His pale, filmed eyes had puffy circles beneath them. His skin looked as though it had never known the sting of a biting wind, nor the warm touch of outdoor sunlight. But those pale, filmed eyes could be coldly insistent, and ten years of hotel management had taught him not to be backward in his demands.

"Now, listen, Doug," he said, "this is just a natural death, see? It isn't suicide. The man took a dose of sleeping medicine, but that didn't have anything to do with his death."

"What's his name?" the district attorney asked.

"The Reverend Charles Brower. He came from Millbank, Nevada. I don't *want* it to be suicide. That gets unpleasant newspaper notoriety for the hotel."

Walking toward the elevator, Selby hoped that the man would at least have tact enough to refrain from referring to campaign obligations, but Cushing's well-manicured, pudgy hand rested on the sleeve of Selby's coat as the door of the elevator opened.

"You know," Cushing said, "I did everything *I* could for you boys during the election, and I'd like to have *you* give *me* the breaks."

Selby nodded.

Cushing said, "The number's three twenty-one," and waved to the elevator operator to close the door.

On the third floor, Selby found no difficulty in locating three twenty-one. He knocked on the panels, and Rex Brandon's voice called, "Is that you, Doug?"

"Yes."

"Go over to three twenty-three, Doug, and come in that way. That door's unlocked."

Selby walked to the adjoining room. It was a typical hotel bedroom. He saw that the connecting door into three twenty-one was ajar. A long sliver had been smashed from the side of the door jamb. Rex Brandon called, "Come on in, Doug."

Selby entered the room.

The little minister seemed strangely wistful as he lay cold and motionless on the bed. The eyes were closed and the jaw had sagged, but the face seemed peaceful, more dignified in death than it had been in life. The door had been locked and a chair propped against it in such a way that the back of the chair was braced directly underneath the knob of the door.

The room seemed filled with silence.

Otto Larkin, big, heavy-voiced chief of police, made haste to greet the district attorney.

"Everything's just as we found it," he assured. "He'd left a call for ten o'clock. The switchboard operator rang and rang and didn't get any answer. A bellboy knocked and heard nothing. He tried a passkey and found the door was bolted from the inside. He climbed up and looked through the transom. He could see the man lying on the bed. He called to him two or three times and then reached inside and pushed down the transom. Then he saw that a chair had been propped under the doorknob. He notified Cushing. Cushing busted in through three twenty-three. That's why the lock's smashed. The connecting door has a double bolt, one on each side.

"Now, listen, Selby, I was pretty friendly with Sam Roper, and I supported him in the campaign. You know that. You can't blame me for it—I'd worked with Sam for four years. But I want to work with you boys, now you're in office. This is the first case we've had, so let's not have any hard feelings that'll keep us from working in harmony. I'd intended to come around and see both of you, but I just hadn't had a chance. There's a lot of things we should talk over."

Selby said, "All right, we'll talk them over at the proper time and in the proper place. What's that paper in the typewriter? It isn't a suicide note, is it?"

"No," Brandon said, "it's a letter to his wife, Doug. Read it, it's sort of pathetic."

Selby stepped over to the table. A portable typewriter held a large sheet of hotel stationery filled with writing.

Selby leaned over the machine and read:

"My DEAREST WIFE:

"Well, I've been in Madison City a couple of days now, and so far haven't accomplished much. I may be here another week, perhaps longer.

"The weather has been perfect. A fine warm sun blazing down from a deep blue sky, windless days and cool nights. It's warm but not hot. The first morning there was a little fog but it didn't last long.

"I'll have a surprise for you when I come back. If I can contact just the right people, we're going to have our financial troubles completely eliminated. And don't think they won't listen to me. They'll *have* to listen. I wasn't born yesterday, you know.

"I didn't sleep well on the train. I had some sleeping medicine to take, but it didn't do much good, so tonight I took a double dose. I think I'm going to sleep fine. In fact, I'm sleepy right now.

"This is a busy city, with a street car line and several nice hotels. It's less than a hundred miles from Hollywood, and I am going to go there before I get back, if I can spare the time. I'm sorry you can't be here with me. I'm getting pretty sleepy now. I think I'll go to bed and finish this in the morning. I'm awfully sleepy, dear. I'll have a nice rest tonight. I'm going to leave a call for ten o'clock in the morning. Tomorrow I'll look around some more.... No use, I'm too sleepy to see the keyboard now."

There followed a word which had been crossed out by x's.

On the table near the typewriter was an envelope addressed to: "*Mrs. Chas. Brower, 613 Center Street, Millbank, Nevada.*"

"Looks as though he took an overdose of the sleeping medicine," Rex Brandon said. "We've checked up on the hotel register. He filled out a card when he checked in. He's Charles Brower and he comes from Millbank, Nevada. He lives at 613 Center Street, the address on the envelope. So everything checks okay. The poor chap wanted to sleep . . . well, he's sleeping all right."

Selby nodded. "Why do you suppose he locked the door and then propped a chair against it?" he asked.

"You can search me," Brandon answered.

The chief of police volunteered a theory. "He was a little guy," he said, "and a minister. Some of those people get timid as rabbits, particularly when they're traveling. Notice the way he talks about the hotels and things. I'll bet he's never done much traveling, and after Millbank this seemed like a big city to him."

"Have you notified the coroner?" Selby asked.

"Yeah, sure. He's out on a funeral right now. We expect him in any minute."

"Look through his things?" Selby asked of Brandon.

"Not yet. We were sort of waiting for the coroner."

"I've been on lots of cases with Harry Perkins, the coroner," Larkin said. "He ain't a bit fussy about red tape. If we want to save time by taking a look through things, it'll be all right with Harry. As a matter of fact, I don't think there's anything to it. He probably had a bum ticker and taking a double dose of sleeping medicine put him out."

"I was wondering," Selby said, "if perhaps he had something very valuable he was trying to guard. I still can't see why he should have gone to all that trouble to lock the door and then prop the chair against it."

He approached the bed and gently raised the corner of the pillow to peer under it. He did this without disturbing the body. Finding nothing, he slid his hand in a fruitless search under the pillow. He turned back the bedclothes, saying, "We might just as well be certain about the cause of death."

The body was attired in a thick flannel nightgown. Selby pulled the bedclothes back up and said, "No sign of any foul play. Well, I guess it's just a routine matter. We'll notify his wife."

"I told George Cushing to send the wife a wire," Sheriff Brandon said. "I wanted her to be notified so she could decide what she wanted done about the body."

The chief of police frowned slightly. "I'm sorry you did that, Sheriff. That's one of the things the coroner likes to do. You know, he's an undertaker, and he usually mentions in his telegrams that he can prepare the body for burial."

The sheriff drawled, "Harry was out on a funeral and I wanted to get some action. He can send her a wire when he comes in, if he wants to."

Selby looked around the room.

The dead man's coat and vest were in the closet, carefully placed on a hanger. The trousers had been caught by the cuffs in the top of the bureau drawer, and hung down almost to the floor. A single suitcase was on the chair, open.

"That's his only baggage?" Selby asked, "a suitcase and a portable typewriter?"

"There's an overcoat and a brief case in the closet," Brandon said.

"What's in the brief case?" Selby asked.

"Just some newspaper clippings and some typewritten stuff—a sermon or a story or something—a lot of words slung together."

"Have you looked through the pockets of his clothes?"

"No."

"Let's do it. You take the clothes and I'll take a look through the suitcase. I can't help thinking he must have had something valuable with him, or he wouldn't have barricaded that door. His letter intimates as much."

The suitcase, Selby found, was packed with scrupulous care. The garments were neatly folded. He noticed two clean shirts, some light underwear, several starched collars, a worn, leather-backed Bible, a pair of spectacles in a case bearing the imprint of a San Francisco oculist, and a half dozen pairs of plain black socks. He saw an oblong pasteboard medicine box with a label on which had been written in pen and ink, *"For Restlessness."* There was also a leather case containing an expensive, foreign-made miniature camera.

"Hello," Selby said, "this is a pretty good outfit for a small town minister to be sporting. They cost about a hundred and fifty dollars."

"Lots of people like this guy was are camera fiends," the chief of police pointed out. "A man has to have some hobby, you know. God knows, his clothes are shiny enough, and the overcoat's badly worn at the elbows."

"Where was his wallet?" Selby asked.

"In his coat pocket," Brandon said.

"Any cards?"

"Yes, a few printed cards bearing the name, 'Charles Brower, D.D., Millbank, Nevada,' ninety-six dollars in cash, and about two dollars in small silver. There's also a driving license."

Selby looked once more at the still figure on the bed.

Somehow, a feeling of indecency gripped him. The man had been a human being, had had his hopes, fears, ambitions, disappointments, and now Selby was prying into his private life. . . . Only the official obligation of discharging his duty prevented him from being a sublimated Peeping Tom.

He found himself wondering how physicians must feel when they are called upon to make intimate examinations of people who are utter strangers, yet must bare the innermost secrets of their lives. Of a sudden, he felt completely fed up.

"All right," he said, "I guess there's nothing to it. Have the coroner take charge. He'll probably want an inquest. By the way, George Cushing would appreciate it if there was no publicity or talk of suicide. It's just a natural death."

He turned away toward the door of three twenty-one, noticed the splintered casing where the bolt had been forced, and said casually, "What's the room on the other side, Rex?"

"I suppose the same as this," the sheriff remarked.

"I think it has a bath," the chief of police volunteered. "The way the hotel is laid out, there's a bath in between rooms, and the room can be rented either with or without a bath. This room didn't have the bath connected with it, so the bath's probably connected with the other room. There's a wash-stand with running water. He has his shaving things over there, see?"

Selby noticed the wash-stand, with a glass shelf above it, on which reposed a shaving brush, the bristles of which had been worn down from much use. In addition to the brush, the shelf held a safety razor, a tube of shaving cream, a tooth brush and a can of tooth powder.

Selby idly inspected the knurled knob on the door which led to the shut-off bathroom. He twisted the knob and said, "Let's see if this door's open on the other side."

Suddenly he frowned, and said, "Wait a minute, this door wasn't bolted. Did someone twist this knob?"

"I don't think so," Larkin said. "The bellboy reported to Cushing and Cushing told everyone nothing in the room was to be touched."

"Then why didn't Cushing get in through three nineteen? He could have unlocked the door from the other side and wouldn't have had to force the other one open."

"I think that room's occupied," Larkin said. "Cushing told me three twenty-three was vacant, but someone's in three nineteen."

Selby nodded and said, "Well, I'm going back to the office. I guess there's nothing I can do here."

A knock sounded on the door of three twenty-one. Brandon called out, "Who is it?"

"Harry Perkins, the coroner."

"Go around to three twenty-three, Harry, and come in that way."

A moment later the tall figure of the bony-faced coroner came through the connecting door.

Larkin made explanations.

"We were just looking around a bit, Harry. You were out on a funeral and we wanted to make sure what it was. It's just a combination of an overdose of sleeping medicine and a bum pump. There won't be enough of an estate to bother with. He's got about a hundred bucks, which should cover your costs of preparing the body for shipment. The sheriff wired his wife. Perhaps you'd better send her another wire and ask her if she wants you to take charge."

The sheriff said, "I'm sorry, Harry, I didn't know you liked to send those wires yourself."

"That's all right," the coroner said. He walked over to the bed, looked down at the still form with a professional air and asked, "When do I move him?"

"Any time," Larkin said. "Ain't that right, Sheriff?"

Brandon looked questioningly at Selby, who nodded.

"I'm going back to the office," Selby said.

"Got a car?" the sheriff asked.

"Yes, thanks. See you fellows later."

3

Douglas Selby cleaned up the more urgent correspondence on his desk, went to a picture show, lay in bed and read a detective story. Reading the mystery yarn, he suddenly realized that it held a personal message for him.

Murder had ceased to be an impersonal matter of technique by which a writer used a corpse merely to serve as a peg on which to hang a mystery. Somehow, the quiet form of the wistful little minister lying in the hotel bedroom pushed its way into his mind, dominated his thoughts.

Selby closed the book with a slap. Why the devil, he thought, was the little minister insidiously dominant in death? In life, the man, with his painfully precise habits, quiet, self-effacing, almost apologetic manner, would never have given Selby any mental reaction other than, perhaps, an amused curiosity.

Selby prided himself upon being a red-blooded, meat-eating fighter. He knew he had gone into the district attorney-ship battle primarily because of the fight involved.

It had not been because he wanted to be district attorney. It was most certainly not because he wanted the salary. He had, of course, as a citizen, noticed certain signs of corruption in the preceding administration. He had seen that the taxpayers wanted a change. Nothing had ever been proven against Sam Roper, but plenty had been surmised. There had been ugly rumors which had been gradually magnified until the time had become ripe for someone to come forward and lead the fight. And the fact that Selby had been the one to lead that fight was caused more by a desire to do battle than by any wish to better the county administration.

Selby switched out the light and tried to sleep, but the thought of what he had seen in that hotel bedroom persisted in his mind. Despite himself, he found his mind reviewing the inanimate objects in that room, as though they had been definite clews pointing toward some disquieting conclusion.

He thought of the deductive reasoning of the hero in the detective novel, and the disquieting thoughts became more persistent. He looked at his watch. It was nearly midnight.

He tried to sleep and couldn't, and even his futile attempt at slumber reminded him of the apologetic little man who had sought to woo sleep with a sedative. At twelve-thirty he put his pride to one side and called Rex Brandon on the telephone.

"Rex," he said, "you're probably going to laugh at me, but I can't sleep."

"What's the matter, Doug?"

"I can't get over that minister."

"What minister?"

"You know, the one we found in the hotel bedroom."

"What about him, Doug, what's the matter?"

"I can't understand why he should have barricaded the door from the corridor, yet neglected to turn the knob in the door which communicated with the bathroom of three nineteen."

Brandon's voice sounded incredulous. "For God's sake, Doug, are you *really* worrying about that, or are you kidding me?"

"No, I'm serious."

"Why, forget it. The man died from an overdose of sleeping medicine. The stuff he was taking was in that pasteboard box. Perkins, the coroner, used to be a druggist, you know. He knew the stuff. This little preacher took too much, and his heart just gave out. It probably would have, sooner or later, anyway. This sleeping medicine just helped things along a bit, that's all."

"But why did he barricade his door as well as lock it?"

"He wasn't accustomed to traveling. Perhaps it's the first time in years he'd been away from home."

"But that business of the pants being held in place in the bureau drawer," Douglas persisted. "That's an old trick of the veteran traveling salesman. No man who'd never been away from home would have done that."

The sheriff laughed. "Just to show you how far you've missed *that* bet," he said, "the man's wife called up the coroner this afternoon. She's coming on by plane. She told Perkins Brower carried five thousand in insurance, and she seems to want to collect that in a hurry. She's due here in the morning. Seems she's a second wife, been widowed once before. She said her husband hadn't been feeling well lately and the doctor had advised a complete rest, so he took his flivver to go out camping. He'd been soliciting funds for a new church and had raised almost enough money to start the building, but it had been too much of a strain on him, and his nerves had given way a bit. She thinks he must have had some mental trouble, to wind up here, because he'd never done any traveling to speak of, and only went into Reno about once a year. She said he was frightened to death of that city. So *that* shows your pants theory is all wet."

Selby laughed apologetically and said, "I guess it's because we saw him in the hotel when he rode down in the elevator with us. Somehow, I couldn't get over the feeling that if there had been . . . well, you know what I mean, Rex . . . oh, well, forget it. I'm sorry I bothered you."

The sheriff laughed and said, "Better take two or three days and go fishing yourself, Doug. That campaign was pretty strenuous for a young chap like you."

Selby laughed, said perhaps he would, and hung up the telephone. He suddenly snapped the receiver back off the hook to ask, "How much money did she say he'd collected?"

The buzzing sound of the wire made him realize that the sheriff had hung up the telephone.

Selby grinned sheepishly, once more dropped the receiver back on the hook and fought with sleep for an hour. When he finally did relax into slumber, it was a sleep which started with nightmare dreams in which the little parson, his face still dark with death, challenged the detective in the mystery novel to a duel to be fought with portable typewriters and sleeping draughts. This sleep finally merged into a dead stupor, from which Selby emerged to grope mechanically for the jangling telephone.

It was broad daylight. Birds were singing in the trees. The sun was streaming through his windows, dazzling his sleep-swollen eyes. He put the receiver to his ear, said, "Hello," and heard Rex Brandon's voice, sounding curiously strained.

"Doug," he said, "something's gone wrong. I wonder if you can get over to your office right away?"

Selby flashed a glance at the electric clock in his bedroom. The hour was 8:30. He strove to keep the sleep out of his voice. "Certainly," he said, making his tone crisply efficient. "It will be about half an hour."

"We'll be waiting for you," Brandon said, and hung up.

Selby wasn't fully awake until two minutes later, when he sent a needle spray of cold water over his body. Then he realized that he wanted most desperately to know what it was that had gone wrong. But it was too late to ask now. Evidently it had been something Brandon didn't want to discuss over the telephone.

He gave himself a quick shave, breakfasted on a can of tomato juice, climbed into his car and reached his office on the stroke of nine.

Amorette Standish, his secretary, said, "The sheriff and a woman are in your private office."

He nodded. Entering his private office, his eyes focused

immediately upon a matronly, broad-hipped, ample-breasted woman of some fifty years, whose gloved hands were folded on her lap. Her eyes surveyed him with a certain quiet capability. There was the calm of cold determination about her.

Rex said, "This is Mary Brower, from Millbank, Nevada. She arrived in Los Angeles by plane early this morning and came here on the bus."

Selby bowed and said, "It's too bad about your husband, Mrs. Brower. It must have come as very much of a shock to you. I'm sorry there wasn't any way we could have broken the news gently . . ."

"But he wasn't my husband," the woman interrupted, with the simple finality of one announcing a very definite and self-evident fact.

"Then you have flown here from Nevada because of a mistake?" Selby asked. "That certainly is . . ."

He stopped mid-sentence. "Good Lord," he said, and sat down in the swivel chair beside his desk to stare dazedly from the woman to Rex Brandon's frowning countenance.

"You see," the sheriff explained, "he had cards and a driving license in his wallet, and there was a letter he'd started to write to you, so we thought, of course, he was Charles Brower."

"He *isn't* my husband," the woman insisted in the same tone of dogged finality. "I never saw him in my life."

"But," Selby pointed out, his mind groping through a sudden maze of contradictory facts, "why should he have written you if . . . How did he sign the register in the hotel, Rex?"

"As the Reverend Charles Brower, 613 Center Street, Millbank, Nevada."

Selby reached for his hat. "Come on, Rex," he said. "We're going down to get to the bottom of this thing."

The woman in the faded brown suit, with brown gloved hands still folded upon her lap, said, with dogged determination, "He is *not* my husband. Who's going to pay my traveling expenses from Nevada here? Don't think I'll quietly turn around and go home without getting paid my carfare, because I won't. I suppose I really could make serious trouble, you know. It was a great shock to me."

4

A trimly efficient young woman clad in a serviceable tailored suit sat waiting in the outer office as Selby started out.

"Hello, Sylvia," he said. "Did you want to see me?"

"Yes."

"I'm frightfully busy right now. I'll see you sometime this afternoon."

"Sometime this afternoon won't do," she told him.

"Why not?"

Her laughing, reddish-brown eyes smiled up at him, but there was a touch of determination about her jaw. "You are now talking," she said, "to Miss Sylvia Martin, a reporter on *The Clarion*, who has been ordered to get an interview or else."

"But can't it wait, Sylvia?"

"Not a chance," she told him.

"But, hang it, it'll *have* to wait."

She turned resignedly toward the door and said, "Oh,

all right, if that's your attitude, of course I'm not running the paper. My boss sent me out to get the interview, and *he* said it was vitally important; that if you wouldn't cooperate with us . . . well, you know how he is—If you want to antagonize him, it's all right with me."

The sheriff frowned at Selby and said, "Of course, Doug, *I* could start investigating this thing and . . ."

Selby sighed, turned back toward his office and said, "Okay, come on in, Sylvia."

She laughed when the door of his private office had clicked shut behind them. "Forgive me for lying, Doug?" she asked.

About what?"

"About being sent to get an interview."

"Weren't you?"

"No, I was just playing a hunch."

His face showed swift annoyance.

"Now don't be like that," she told him, "because it isn't nice. Don't take the duties of your office too seriously."

"Snap out of it, Sylvia," he told her. "Just what are you trying to do? I'm working on an important case, and you've thrown me off my stride."

She crossed her knees, smoothed her skirt, produced a notebook and pencil and started making intricate little patterns on the upper left-hand corner of the page. "You know, Doug," she said, "*The Clarion* supported you in the campaign. *The Blade* fought you. We want the breaks."

"You'll get them as soon as there are any breaks."

"How about this minister's wife?" she asked. "I've heard she won't identify the body."

"Where did you get that idea?"

"A little bird told me."

"Well, he asked, "what of it?"

Her eyes rested steadily on his. "Doug," she said slowly, "you know what an awful thing it would be, if some important case turned up right at the start and you muffed it."

He nodded. "What makes you think I'm muffing it, Sylvia?"

"Call it womanly intuition, if you want. You know how hard I worked for you during the campaign, and how proud I am you're elected. I . . ."

He laughed, and said, "Okay, Sylvia, you win. Here's the low-down. That woman was Mrs. Mary Brower, of Millbank, Nevada, and she says the body isn't that of her husband. And she's inclined to be peeved about everything."

"Where does that leave you?" she asked.

"Frankly," he told her, "I don't know."

"But didn't the dead man have a letter in his typewriter plainly addressed to his dear wife? And wasn't the envelope addressed to Mrs. Charles Brower at Millbank?"

"That's right," Doug admitted.

"And what does *that* mean?"

"It might mean either one of two things," Selby said slowly. "If the man who regiestered as Brower wanted to impress some visitor that he really *was* Brower, it would have been quite natural for him to write this letter and leave it in the typewriter as a part of the deception. Then he might have left the room for a moment, figuring his visitor would read the letter while he was gone."

Sylvia Martin nodded her head slowly and said, "Yes,

that's right. Let me see if I can guess the other alternative, Doug."

"I wish you would," he told her. "It's got me stumped. It's so wildly improbable and yet so thoroughly logical that . . ."

She held up her hand for silence, frowned at him in thoughtful concentration for a moment, then suddenly exclaimed, "I've got it."

"What is it?"

"If someone was in the room *after* the man had died and wanted to make it appear the cause of death was an overdose of sleeping medicine, he couldn't have hit on a better scheme than to write a letter like that and leave it in the typewriter. The natural person to whom such a letter should be written would be the man's wife, and, if he'd thought the man was Charles Brower, of Millbank, he'd have . . ."

"Exactly," Selby interrupted. "Thank Heavens you agree with me on that. It seemed such a bizarre theory that I couldn't even entertain it."

"But, if that's true," she pointed out, "the man who wrote the letter must have known the wife. Otherwise, he couldn't have known the street address."

Selby said, "No, the man *could* have gotten the address from the hotel registrations. However, supposing he didn't, let's now take a look at Mary Brower, a matronly, capable woman who certainly wouldn't be cavorting around with people who'd want to murder her husband. She's obstinate, perhaps a bit selfish, but certainly no Cleopatra."

Sylvia Martin was staring at him with wide, fascinated eyes. "But let's suppose you're wrong, Doug. Suppose someone *did* know her rather well and wanted her husband out of the way. Suppose this dead man sensed something of the situation and was a close friend of the husband. The husband didn't know anything at all about what was going on, so this friend came to the hotel to take the part of the husband, and in order to do so masqueraded as Charles Brower."

Selby said slowly, "That's a nice theory, Sylvia, and if you publish any part of it, your newspaper will be defendant in about a dozen libel suits. This Mrs. Brower looks like a perfectly capable woman."

Sylvia left her chair and came to stand by his desk.

"Listen, Doug," she said, "my boss got a straight tip that *The Blade* is laying for you on this case. Don't muff it, Doug. Keep your head and out-smart them."

"You mean *The Blade* knows something?" Selby asked.

"I don't know *what* they know, but we've got a tip they're going to stir up some trouble about this case. You know Otto Larkin, the chief of police, is friendly with the managing editor. *I* think Larkin would double-cross you in a minute, if he had a chance. Any stuff *The Blade* has must have come from him."

"Larkin isn't any Sherlock Holmes," Selby pointed out.

"Just the same," she said, "I've given you the tip. Tell me, Doug, will you let me know if anything new develops?"

"I won't release any information for publication until I'm satisfied it won't hamper a solution of the case," he said slowly.

"But can't you just talk things over with me, not for publication, and let me have something to say about whether it's safe to publish them?"

"Well," he told her, "we might do that. But, in the meantime, I've got to get to work."

She closed her notebook and said, "It's definite then that this Mrs. Brower inists the man is not her husband?"

He nodded.

"And," she asked him slowly, "how do you know that *this* woman *is* Mrs. Brower?"

He eyed her speculatively for a moment and said, "Now *that's* a thought."

"I think," she told him, "we can find out from our Nevada correspondents."

"And I," he told her, "will also do a little investigating."

He saw her to the door, then said to Amorette Standish, "Take a wire to the chief of police at Millbank, Nevada, asking him for a description of the Reverend Charles Brower and of Mary Brower his wife. Also find out if he knows where both of them are at present. Tell him to wire."

5

Selby strode into the coroner's office and said, "Harry, I want to go over everything you took from that minister's room."

"The stuff is sealed up and in this room over here," the coroner told him. "Funny thing about putting a wrong tag on him, wasn't it? What a sweet spot I'd have been in, if I'd sent the body by express to Nevada."

Selby said, "Well, either *he* wasn't Charles Brower, or *she* isn't Mary Brower. She looks genuine. You get Dr. Trueman to make an examination. And I want a thorough examination made. Have the contents of the stomach analyzed and analyze all of the vital organs to find traces of poison."

"You don't think it's anything like *that*, do you?" the coroner protested.

"I don't know what I think. I'm going to find out when I've got something to think on."

"Aw, shucks, it's just a case of mistaken identity. It'll

be all straightened out within another twenty-four hours. His heart went back on him, and that's all there was to it. I used to see plenty of cases like that when I was running my drug store . . ."

"Nevertheless," Selby said, "I want to know just how the man died."

"Just knowing that his identity is mixed up doesn't make any difference in the *way* the man died," the coroner said in a slow, protesting drawl. "I wouldn't get all steamed up about it, if I were you, Douglas."

"I'm not steamed up," the district attorney said. "I'm getting busy."

He took the suitcase, the portable typewriter and the brief case which the coroner handed him.

Selby said, "I think you'd better sit in here with me, Harry, and make a list of all this stuff."

"I've already listed it," the coroner replied.

"How did you describe it?"

"Personal papers, newspaper clippings and such stuff."

"I think we'd better make a more detailed list."

"Well, you go ahead and make it out. Anything you say is okay."

"I'd prefer to have you with me while we went over it."

"I'm awfully busy now, Doug . . . But I can, if you want."

"I'll just hit the high spots," the district attorney promised, "but I want to know everything that's in here."

He sat down in the chair, cut the sealed tape, opened the brief case and took out a number of papers from the leather pockets. He started sorting the newspaper clippings.

"Here's one of Shirley Arden, the motion picture star," he said, "showing her in her new play, *Mended Hearts*. Here's another one of her in a 'still' taken during the filming of that picture. Here's one of her in *Page the Groom*. Here's some publicity about her from one of the motion picture fan magazines. Why all the crush on Shirley Arden, Harry?"

The coroner said, "That's nothing. We see that every day. Almost everyone has some favorite motion picture star. People collect all sorts of stuff. You remember this chap said in his letter that he might go on to Hollywood? I'll bet you he's gone on Shirley Arden, and was hoping he'd have a chance to meet her."

The district attorney, forced to accept the logic of the remark, nodded, turned to the rest of the papers.

"Hello," he said, "here's some newspaper clippings about the Perry Estate. I wonder if he's interested in that?"

"I was wondering about that, too," the coroner said. "I just took a quick look through them. That's the Perry Estate that's being fought over in our Superior Court, isn't it? It says the man who's trying to prove he's the heir is H. F. Perry. That'll be Herbert Perry, won't it?"

Selby read through the clippings and nodded.

"They aren't clippings from our papers, are they?"

"No. They're Associated Press dispatches, sent out to a number of papers which subscribe for that service."

"Why do you suppose he saved them?"

"That's one of the things we're going to find out."

"What are they fighting about in that case, anyway?"

"Charles Perry," Selby said, "was married and got an

interlocutory decree of divorce. Then, before the final decree was issued, he went over to Yuma and married an Edith Fontaine. At the time of the marriage she had a son, Herbert. Herbert took the name of Perry, but Charles Perry wasn't his father. The marriage, having been performed while an interlocutory decree was in effect, and before a final decree had been entered, was void. That was years ago. Apparently Perry never knew his marriage wasn't legal. His first wife died, but he never had another marriage ceremony with Edith. He died without a will, and his brother, H. Franklin Perry, is contesting Herbert Perry's share in the estate."

"Isn't there some law about marriage not being necessary where people live openly as man and wife?"

"That's a common-law marriage," Selby said. "It doesn't apply in this state."

"Well, Perry *thought* he was married to her all right. He died first, didn't he?"

"Yes, they were in an automobile accident. He was killed instantly. She lived for a week with a fractured skull and died."

"So the boy doesn't get any of the money?" Perkins asked. "I know the brother. He's a veterinary. He treated my dog for distemper once. He's a good man."

"Who gets the money is something for the courts to decide," Selby said. "What I'm wondering about right now is what interested Charles Brower in that particular case."

"Do you think he was Brower?"

"No, Harry, I don't. I'm just calling him that because I don't know anything else to call him. I'd like to find out what paper these were cut from. There's nothing to indicate, is there?"

The coroner shook his head.

Selby looked through other clippings. One of them, from a fan magazine, listed the motion picture actors and actresses in the order of their popularity. Another one gave what purported to be a tabulation of the gross earnings of the various stars during the preceding year.

A second pocket in the brief case contained a sheaf of typewritten papers. Evidently the typewriting had been done on the minister's portable typewriter. It was a ragged job filled with crossed-out words and strike-overs. The district attorney noticed that at the top of page one appeared a title reading *"Lest Ye Be Judged."* There followed a story written in laborious, pedantic style. Selby started to wade through the story. Despite himself, it was impossible for him to read without skipping whole paragraphs at a time. It was the story of an old, irascible judge, entirely out of sympathy with the youth of the day, who had passed a harsh judgment upon a delinquent girl who had come before him. The judgment had been entirely without understanding and without mercy. The girl, declared to be an incorrigible, had been sentenced to a reformatory, but friends rallied to her support, led by a man whose status was not entirely clear. He was referred to as a lover of humanity.

The district attorney, searching the manuscript for some clew which would indicate this man's love might have had a more personal focal point, became lost in a maze of pointless writing. He finally gathered that the man was much older; that his love was, in fact, really impersonal. The girl took up the study of medicine in the second chapter and became a noted surgeon before the third.

In chapter three, the judge's granddaughter, suffering with a brain tumor, was taken to the "greatest specialist in the world," and when the judge, tears streaming down his face, called to plead with the surgeon to do his best, he found that the surgeon was none other than the girl he had sentenced as an incorrigible.

There were several pages of psychological explanations, the general purport of which was that the girl had been filled with a certain excess of vitality, a certain animal energy which required a definite ambition upon which to concentrate. The man who had saved her had been shrewd enough to place her in school and to dare her to accomplish the impossible. The very difficulty of the task had served to steady her.

"What's it about?" the coroner asked, when the district attorney had turned over the last page.

"It's a proof of the old axiom," Selby said, grinning.

"What axiom?"

"That there lives no man with soul so dead, who hasn't tried to write a picture scenario."

"That what is it?"

"That's what it was probably intended to be."

"I'll bet you he figured on going down to Hollywood to peddle that scenario."

"If he did," Selby pointed out, "he certainly made a peculiar detour. He was sneaking into Hollywood by the back way."

There were no further papers in the brief case. The district attorney closed it and the coroner taped and sealed it.

Once more Selby went into the suitcase.

"There aren't any laundry marks on any of those clothes," the coroner said. "Not even on his starched collars. Ain't that a little peculiar?"

Selby nodded.

"Probably the first trip he'd made with these clothes," he said, "or he'd have had them laundered somewhere. And he couldn't have been away from home very long. Also, he must have a very efficient wife who's a hard-working housekeeper. That all indicates a ministerial background."

Selby inspected the small pasteboard box containing a long roll of paper in which five-grain tablets had been folded.

"This the sedative?" he asked.

"Yes."

"And one of these tablets wouldn't have brought about death?"

"Not a chance," the coroner said. "I've known people to take four of them."

"What *did* cause death then?"

"Probably a bad heart. A double dose of this stuff might have helped bring on the heart attack."

"You have Dr. Trueman check carefully on that heart attack," Selby instructed. "I want to know, absolutely, what caused this man's death."

The coroner fidgeted uneasily, finally said, "I wonder

if you'd mind if I gave you a little advice, Douglas."

"Go ahead, Harry, dish it out," Selby said with a smile, "and I'll try and take it."

"This is your first case," the coroner said. "You seem to be trying to make a murder case out of it. Now I wouldn't go putting the cart before the horse. There's a lot of sentiment against you in this county, and a lot of it for you. The people who are for you put you in office. The people who are against you hate to have you in office. You go along without attracting any great amount of attention for a month or two, and pretty quick people will forget all about the political end of things. Then those who hated you will be smiling and shaking hands when they see you on the street. But, you get off on the wrong foot, and it's going to hurt. Your enemies will be tickled to death and you'll lose some of your friends."

Selby said, "Harry, I don't care how this thing looks to you, *I'm* not satisfied with it. There are lots of things about it I'm not satisfied with."

"You get to looking at dead people through a microscope and you'll never be satisfied with anything," the coroner objected. "Things never do check out in real life. I've seen lots of deaths that couldn't be explained; that is, some things didn't look as though they could possibly fit in with other things. But you learn to take cases for granted, after a while. This guy was registered under a phony name, that's all. Nothing to get excited about in that—lots of people do it."

Selby shook his head and laid down what was to be his primary code of conduct during his term of office.

"Harry," he said, "facts fit. They're like figures. If you

get all the facts, your debit column adds up the same as your credit column. The facts balance with the result and the result balances with the facts. Any time they don't, it's because we haven't all of the facts, and are trying to force a balance with the wrong figures. Now take that type-written letter, for instance. It wasn't written by the same man who wrote the scenario. The typing in the letter is perfect, evenly matched and free of strike-overs. The scenario is a hunt-and-peck affair, sloppy and ragged. Probably they were both written on the same machine, but they weren't written by the same person. That's an illustration of what I mean by saying that facts must balance, if they're going to support theories."

The coroner sighed. "Well, I told you, anyhow," he remarked. "Go ahead and make a murder out of it, if you want to. You'll find it'll be a boomerang."

Selby grinned, thanked him, left the mortuary and went at once to the Madison Hotel.

In the manager's private office Selby had a showdown with George Cushing.

"Otto Larkin," Cushing said reproachfully, "tells me you're making a mountain out of a molehill on this Brower case, Selby. I didn't think you'd do that to me."

"I'm not doing it to you, George."

"Well, you're doing it to my business."

"I'm not doing anything to your business. I'm going to find out the facts in this case, that's all."

"You've already got the facts."

"No, I haven't. The facts I've had have been wrong. The man isn't Charles Brower."

"Oh, that," Cushing said, with a wave of his hand, "that

frequently happens. Lots of people register under assumed names for one reason or another, and sometimes, if people happen to have a friend's card in their pockets, they'll register under the name of the friend, figuring they can produce the card, if anyone questions them.

"I don't know why they do it, because we never pay any attention to names, anyway. We make them put a street address opposite their names on the register, because we want to know where to send things, in case they leave something valuable behind. It gives us a good mailing list and sometimes it's of value against fraud, but not very often."

"Whom did this man know in the hotel?" the district attorney asked.

Cushing raised his eyebrows. "In the hotel?" he asked. "Why, I don't suppose he knew anyone."

"Whom did he know in town?"

"I couldn't tell you about that. No one that I know of. A man who hadn't done much traveling and came here from Millbank, Nevada, wouldn't be apt to know anyone here in the hotel, or in the town, either."

"When Sheriff Brandon and I were coming out of campaign headquarters on the fifth floor the other morning," Selby said, "this preacher was coming out of a room on the fifth floor. It was a room on the right-hand side of the corridor, and I'd say it was somewhere between five-o-seven and five nineteen."

Cushing's face showed emotion. He leaned forward. His breathing was distinctly audible.

"Now, listen, Doug," he said, "why not lay off of this

thing? You're not doing the hotel any good and you're not doing yourself any good."

"I'm going to find out who this man is and I'm going to find out how he died and why he died," Selby said doggedly.

"He's some bird from Millbank, Nevada, or some nearby place," Cushing said. "He knows this man Brower in Millbank. He knew Brower was away on a fishing trip, so he figured it would be a good time to use Brower's name."

"Who occupied those rooms on the fifth floor?" Selby insisted.

"I'm sure I couldn't tell you."

"Get your register."

"Now, listen, Doug, you're carrying this thing too far."

The district attorney said, "Get the register, George."

"We keep the register in the form of cards."

"How do you file those cards?"

"Alphabetically."

"Then you copy them somewhere into a daily register. Go get it."

Cushing got up, started for the door, hesitated for a moment, then came back and sat down.

"Well," Selby said, "go ahead, get the register."

"There's something about this," Cushing said slowly, "that I don't want made public. It doesn't concern this case in any way."

"What is it?"

"It's something that won't be shown by the register, but you'll probably find out about it, if you get to nosing around. . . . And," he added bitterly, "it looks like you're going to nose around."

"I am," Selby promised.

"There was a guest here Monday who didn't want her identity known."

"What room was she in?"

"Five fifteen."

"Who was she?"

"I can't tell you that, Doug. It hasn't anything to do with the case."

"Why don't you want to tell me then?"

"Because she came here on business. It was rather a confidential business. She was trying to keep it from becoming known. She signed a fictitious name on the register and made me agree I'd say nothing about her having been here. She only stayed a couple of hours and then went back. Her manager, I think, stayed on a little longer."

"Who was she?"

"I can't tell you. She's famous and she didn't want the newspapers making a lot of hullabaloo about her. I don't want her to think I've broken my promise. She comes here sometimes when she wants to get away from everything, and always has the same room. I sort of keep it for her . . . and . . . well, that's why I'm telling you all this. I don't want you stirring up any publicity about room five fifteen."

An idea suddenly crystallized in Selby's mind, an idea so weirdly bizarre that it didn't make sense, yet was entirely on a par with the other developments in the case.

"That woman," he said with the calm finality of one

who is absolutely certain of his statements, "was Shirley Arden, the motion picture actress."

George Cushing's eyes widened. "How the devil did you know?"

Selby said, "Never mind that. Tell me all you know."

"Ben Trask, her manager and publicity agent, was with her. Miss Arden went in by way of the freight elevator. Trask saw that the coast was clear."

"Did anyone in the hotel call on her?"

"I wouldn't know."

"Did Trask have a room here?"

"No."

"What is this room, a bedroom?"

"It's a suite; a bedroom, sitting room and bath."

"Any outside telephone calls?" Selby asked.

"I wouldn't know. I can find out by looking up the records."

"Do that."

Cushing fidgeted uneasily and said, "This preacher left an envelope in the safe. I had forgotten about it until this morning. Do you want me to get it?"

"What's in it?"

"A letter or something."

"Yes," Selby said, "get it."

"I'd like to have you sign for it."

"All right, bring a receipt and I'll sign."

The hotel manager stepped from the office for a few moments, then returned with a sealed envelope, across the flap of which appeared a scrawled signature, "Charles Brower."

"That his writing?" Selby asked.

"I think so, yes."

"Have you checked it with his signature on the register?"

"No, but I can."

"Wait here," Selby told him, "while I open the envelope. We'll list the contents."

He slit the end of the envelope with a knife and pulled out several folded sheets of hotel stationery.

"Well," he said, "this looks..."

His voice trailed into silence as his fingers unfolded the sheets of stationery. Five one-thousand-dollar bills had been folded between two sheets of hotel stationery.

"Good Lord!" Cushing exclaimed.

"You sure the minister put this envelope in the safe?" Selby asked.

"Yes."

"No chance for any mistake?"

"None whatever."

Selby turned the bills over in his fingers. Then, as a delicate scent was wafted to his nostrils, he raised the bills to his nose; pushed them across the table and said to Cushing, "Smell."

Cushing sniffed the bills. "Perfume," he said.

Selby folded the bills back in the paper and slipped both paper and bills back in the envelope.

"Take a strip of gummed paper," he said. "Seal up that envelope and put it back in the safe. That'll keep the odor of the perfume from being dissipated. I'll want to check it later.... Now, then, who had room three nineteen?"

"Where the body was discovered, a man by the name of Block was in the room"

"Where's he from? What does he do, and how long have you known him?"

"He's a traveling salesman who works for one of the hardware firms in Los Angeles. He comes here every month and works the outlying towns and the dealers here, usually makes a two-day stand."

"Has he checked out yet?"

"I don't think so, but he's just about due to check out."

"I want to talk with him."

"I'll see if he's in."

"Who had the room before Block?"

"I've looked that up. The room hadn't been rented for three days."

"The room on the other side—three twenty-three?"

"That was vacant when the body was discovered, but had been rented the night before to a young couple from Hollywood, a Mr. and Mrs. Leslie Smith."

"Get their street number from the register. See if this salesman is in his room. I want to talk with him. Seal that envelope and put it back in the safe."

Cushing excused himself, and this time was gone some five minutes. He returned, accompanied by a well-dressed man in the early thirties, whose manner radiated smiling self-assurance.

"This is Mr. Block, the man who's in room three nineteen," he said.

Block wasted no time in preliminaries. His face wreathed in a welcoming smile, he gripped Selby's hand cordially.

"I'm very pleased to meet you, Mr. Selby. I understand you're to be congratualted on winning one of the most bitterly contested elections ever held in the history of the county. I've been covering this territory several years, and I've heard everywhere about the splendid campaign you were putting up. My name's Carl Block, and I'm with the Central Hardware Supplies Company. I come through here regularly once a month, making headquarters here for a couple of days, while I cover the outlying towns. Is there any way in which I can be of service to you?"

The man was friendly. Sizing him up, Selby knew why he held such a splendid sales record, knew also that it would be next to impossible to surprise any information from him.

"You got in yesterday morning, Mr. Block?"

"That's right."

"About what time?"

"Well, I got in pretty early. I find that these days the business comes to the man who goes after it. My best time to cover the small accounts is between eight and nine-thirty. The small man is opened and swept out about eight. Trade doesn't really start until around nine. The bigger accounts have clerks who open up. The managers get in around nine, have their mail read about nine-thirty, and my best time with them is between nine-thirty and eleven-thirty.

"I'm just telling you this, Mr. Selby, so you'll understand why I got in so early. I'd say I got in about seven o'clock. I left Los Angeles shortly before five, just tumbled out of bed and into the car. After I got up here I bathed, shaved, freshened up a bit, had a cup of coffee and caught my first customer at eight o'clock."

"Hear any unusual sounds from the adjoining room?"

"Not a sound."

"Thank you," Selby said, "that's all." He nodded to Cushing and said, "I'm going back to my office, George. Don't give out any information."

Cushing followed him to the door of the hotel. "Now listen, Doug," he said, "this thing was just a natural death. There's no use getting worked up about it, and, remember to keep that information about Miss Arden under your hat."

6

Selby said to Frank Gordon, "Frank, I want you to find out everything you can about the litigation in the Perry Estate."

"I think I can tell you all about it," Gordon said. "I know John Baggs, the attorney for Herbert Perry. He's discussed the case with me."

"What are the facts?"

"Charles Perry married Edith Fontaine in Yuma. The marriage wasn't legal because Perry only had an interlocutory decree. He had the mistaken idea he could leave the state and make a good marriage. Edith Fontaine had a son by a previous marriage—Herbert Fontaine—he changed his name to Perry. Perry and his wife were killed in an auto accident. If there wasn't any marriage, the property goes to H. Franklin Perry, the veterinary, a brother of Charles. If the marriage was legal, the bulk of the property vested in Edith on the death of Charles, and Herbert is Edith's sole heir. That's the case in a nutshell."

"Who's representing H. Franklin Perry?"

"Fred Lattaur."

"Get a picture of the dead minister. See if either of the litigants can identify him."

He picked up the phone and said to the exchange operator, "I want Sheriff Brandon, please. Then I want Shirley Arden, the picture actress." He held the line, and a moment later heard Rex Brandon's voice.

"Just had an idea," Selby said. "There were a pair of reading spectacles in that suitcase. Get an oculist here to get the prescription. Get a photograph of the dead man. Rush the photograph and the prescription to the oculist in San Francisco, whose name is on the spectacle case. Have him look through his records and see if he can identify the spectacles."

"Shall I tell him the man's a minister?" Brandon asked.

"Right now," Selby said, "it looks as though he's more apt to have been a gangster or a racketeer of some sort, perhaps a damn clever blackmailer. Get hold of Cushing over at the hotel and get an earful of the latest developments. Then, when you get a chance, get in touch with me and we'll talk things over. I'm trying to locate a certain party in Hollywood."

"Okay," Brandon said cheerfully. "I'm running down a couple of other clews. I'll see you later on."

Selby's secretary reported, "Miss Arden is working on the set. She can't come to the telephone. A Mr. Trask says he'll take the call. He says he's her manager."

"Very well," Selby said, "put Trask on the line."

"He heard a click, then a masculine voice saying suavely, "Yes, hello, Mr. Selby."

Selby snapped words into the transmitter. "I don't want

to say anything over the telephone which would embarrass you or Miss Arden," he said. "Perhaps you know who I am."

"Yes, I do, Mr. Selby."

"Day before yesterday," Selby said, "Miss Arden made a trip. You were with her."

"Yes."

"I want to question her about that trip."

"But why?"

Selby said, "I think you'd prefer I didn't answer that question over the telephone. I want to see both you and Miss Arden in my office sometime before nine o'clock tonight."

"But, I say, that's quite impossible," Trask protested. "Miss Arden's working on a picture and . . ."

"She won't be working straight through until nine o'-clock tonight," Selby interrupted.

"Well, it'll be rather late this afternoon when she finishes, and she'll be tired."

"I can understand that very well," Selby retorted, "but this matter is sufficiently important for me to insist upon her presence."

"But it can't be important enough to . . ."

Selby interrupted. "I have ways," he said, "of getting Miss Arden's statement. There are hard ways and easy ways. This is the easy way—for you."

There was a moment's silence, during which the district attorney could hear the man at the other end of the telephone breathing heavily. Then the voice said, "At ten o'-clock tonight, Mr. Selby?"

"I'd prefer an earlier hour. How about seven or eight?"

"Eight o'clock would be the earliest time we could possibly make it. Miss Arden, you know, is under contract, and . . ."

"Very well," Selby said, "at eight o'clock tonight," and hung up before the manager could think of additional excuses.

He had hardly hung up the telephone before it rang with shrill insistence. He took the receiver from the hook, said, "Hello," and heard the calmly professional voice of Dr. Ralph Trueman.

"You wanted information about that man who was found dead in the Madison Hotel," Trueman said.

"Yes, Doctor, What information have you?"

"I haven't covered everything," Dr. Trueman said, "but I've gone far enough to be morally certain of the cause of death."

"What was it?"

"A lethal dose of morphine, taken internally."

"Of morphine!" Selby exclaimed. "Why, the man had some sleeping tablets . . ."

"Which hadn't been taken at all, so far as I can ascertain," Trueman interrupted. "But what he *had* taken was a terrific dose of morphine, which induced paralysis of the respiratory organs. Death probably took place some time between midnight and three o'clock yesterday morning."

"And when was the morphine administered?"

"Any time from one to two hours prior to death."

"How?"

"Well, I'm not certain about that," Trueman said, "but

there's some chance a tablet containing the deadly dose *might* have been inserted in the box of sedative which the man was carrying with him. In that event he'd have taken the morphia thinking he was taking an ordinary sleeping tablet. The tablets were wrapped in paper so that they'd naturally be taken in a consecutive order. I've made a very delicate test with some of the paper remaining in the box and get a definite trace of morphia."

"Could that have been a possible error on the part of the druggist filling the prescription?" Selby asked.

"In a tablet of that size, with that amount of morphia," Dr. Trueman said, "the chance of honest error would be just about one in ten million."

"Then . . . then it was deliberate, carefully planned murder," Selby exclaimed.

Dr. Trueman's voice retained its professional calm. "That," he observed, "is a matter of law. *I'm* merely giving you the medical facts."

7

Selby rang Sheriff Brandon on the telephone and said, "Have you heard Trueman's report on that Brower case?"

"Yes, I just talked with him. What do you think of it?"

"I think it's murder."

"Listen, Doug," Rex said, "we've got to work fast on this thing. *The Blade* will start riding us."

"That's all right. We've got to expect to be roasted once in a while. But let's chase down all of the clews and see if we can't keep one jump ahead of the knockers. Did you get in touch with the San Francisco oculist?"

"Yes, I sent him a wire."

"Better get him on the telephone and see if you can speed things up any. He may be able to give us some information. Now, here's another thing. Room three twenty-three had been rented to a Mr. and Mrs. Leslie Smith of Hollywood. I told Cushing to get their address from the register. I wish you'd get that information, telephone the

Hollywood police and see if you can get a line on the couple. If you can't, you should be able to wire the motor vehicle department and find out if a Leslie Smith, of Hollywood, owns an automobile, and get his residence from the registration certificate. Also, see if a Leslie Smith had a car stored in one of the garages near the hotel."

"Of course," the sheriff pointed out, "he might have been using a fictitious name."

"Try it, anyway," Selby said. "Let's go through the facts in this case with a fine-tooth comb. They can't expect us to be infallible, Rex. Lots of murders are never solved, even in cities where they have the most efficient police forces. What we have to guard against is slipping up on some little fact where a *Blade* reporter can give us the horse laugh. Figure the position we'll be in if *The Blade* solves this murder while we're still groping around in the dark."

"I get you," Brandon said grimly. "Leave it to me. I'll turn things upside down and inside out."

"One other thing," Selby said. "When you get George Cushing in the sweat box, he'll probably give you some information about a certain picture actress who was in the hotel. You don't need to bother about that. We don't want any publicity on it right at the present time and I've been in touch with her manager. They're going to be up here at eight o'clock tonight at my office. I'll find out if there's anything to it and let you know."

"Okay," Brandon said, "I'll get busy. You stick around and I'll probably have something for you inside of half an hour."

As the district attorney hung up the telephone his secretary brought him a telegram from the chief of police of Millbank, Nevada.

Selby read:

"ANSWERING YOUR WIRE MARY BROWER FIVE FEET FOUR INCHES WEIGHT ONE HUNDRED SIXTY POUNDS AGE AS GIVEN TO REGISTRATION AUTHORITIES FIFTY TWO RESIDES SIX THIRTEEN CENTER STREET THIS CITY LAST SEEN LEAVING FOR RENO TO TAKE PLANE FOR LOS ANGELES REPORTED TO FRIENDS HUSBAND HAD DIED IN SOUTHERN CALIFORNIA WAS WEARING BROWN SUIT BROWN GLOVES DARK BROWN COAT TRIMMED WITH FOX FUR STOP CHARLES BROWER PASTOR METHODIST CHURCH THIS CITY FIVE FEET SEVEN INCHES ONE HUNDRED THIRTY FIVE POUNDS GRAY EYES HIGH CHEEKBONES AGE GIVEN ON CHURCH RECORDS AS FIFTY SIX HEALTH POOR RECENTLY LEFT HERE IN CHEVROLET AUTOMOBILE TWENTY EIGHT MODEL LICENSE SIX FIVE FOUR THREE EIGHT WEARING BLUE SERGE SUIT SOFT COLLAR SHIRT BLUE AND WHITE TIE TAN LOW SHOES HAS SMALL TRIANGULAR SCAR BACK OF RIGHT EAR RESULTING AUTOMOBILE ACCIDENT THREE YEARS AGO STOP WIRE IF ADDITIONAL DETAILS DESIRED."

Selby looked at the wire, nodded and said, "There's a man who knows his job."

Amorette Standish let her curiosity show in her voice. "Were you wondering if she really is Mrs. Brower?"

"I was," he said.

"And the dead man?" she asked. "Was he Mr. Brower?"

"I don't think so. The woman says he isn't, and the description doesn't fit. Ring up the coroner and ask him to look particularly for the small triangular scar mentioned in the wire. I don't think he'll find it, but we'll look anyway."

As his secretary took the telegram and left the room, Selby got to his feet and began a restless pacing of the office. At length he sat down at his desk and started scribbling a wire to the chief of police at Millbank, Nevada.

"Ascertain if possible," he wrote, "if Brower had friend probably a minister between forty-five and fifty-five about five feet five inches weight about hundred and twenty small-boned dark hair gray at temples small round bald spot top and back of head interested in photography probably had made several fruitless attempts to sell scenarios hollywood studios interested in motion pictures last seen wearing black frock coat well worn and shiny black trousers black high shoes stop eyes blue manner very self-effacing enunciation very precise as though accustomed public speaking from pulpit owns royal portable typewriter wire reply earliest available moment important thanks for co-operation."

Selby gave the telegram to Amorette Standish to be sent. His telephone was ringing before she had left the office. He took down the receiver and heard Sheriff Brandon's voice.

"Have some news for you, Doug," the sheriff said.

"Found out who he was?"

"No, not yet."

"Talk with that oculist in San Francisco?"

"Yes. He got my wire but had been pretty busy and had just hit the high spots going over his records. He hadn't found anything. I don't think he'd been trying very hard. I put a bee in his bonnet, told him to check over every prescription he had in his files if necessary. He said the prescription wasn't particularly unusual. I told him to make a list of every patient he had who had that prescription and send me a telegram."

"What else?" Selby asked.

Brandon lowered his voice.

"Listen, Doug," he said cautiously, "the opposition are going to try to put us on the spot."

"Go ahead," Selby said.

"Jerry Summerville, who runs *The Blade*, has imported a crack mystery man from Los Angeles, a fellow by the name of Carl Bittner. He's been a star reporter for some of the Los Angeles dailies. I don't know how much money it cost, or who's putting it up, but Summerville put in the call this morning and Bittner is here in town now. He's been asking questions of the coroner and trying to pump Cushing."

"What did Cushing tell him, do you know?"

"No. He pulled a fast one with Cushing. He said he was a special investigator and sort of gave Cushing to understand he was from your office. Cushing talked a little bit. I don't know how much. . . . Suppose we could throw a scare into this bird for impersonating an officer?"

"Special investigator doesn't mean anything," Selby said

slowly. "Let's go slow on bothering about what the other people are doing, Rex, and solve the case ourselves. After all, we have all the official machinery at our disposal, and we've got a head start."

"Not very much of a head start," the sheriff said. "We collect the facts and the other fellows can use them."

"We don't need to tell them *all* we know," Selby pointed out.

"That's one of the things I wanted to ask you about. Suppose we clamp down the lid on information?"

"That's okay by me."

"All right, we'll do it. Now here's something else for you. Mr. and Mrs. Leslie Smith are phonies. They gave an address of 3350 Blair Drive. There isn't any such number. There are about fifty automobiles registered to Leslie Smiths in various parts of the state."

"Okay," Selby said after a moment, "it's up to you to run down all fifty of those car owners."

"I was talking with Cushing," Brandon went on, "and he says they were a couple of kids who might have been adventuring around a bit and used the first alias that came into their heads."

"Cushing *may* be right," Selby rejoined, "but *we're* solving this case, he isn't. It stands to reason that someone got into the minister's room through one of the adjoining rooms. That chair being propped under the doorknob would have kept the door of three twenty-one from opening. Both doors were locked on three twenty-three. I'm inclined to favor three nineteen."

"But there wasn't anyone in three nineteen."

Selby said, "Let's make absolutely certain of that, Rex.

I don't like the way Cushing is acting in this thing. He's not co-operating as well as he might. Suppose you get hold of him and throw a scare into him?"

"And here's something else," Selby went on. "I noticed that the writing on the letter which had been left in the typewriter was nice neat typewriting, almost professional in appearance."

"I hadn't particularly noticed that," the sheriff said, after a moment, "but I guess perhaps you're right."

"Now then, on the scenario, which was in his brief case," Selby pointed out, "the typing was ragged, the letters in the words weren't evenly spaced. There were lots of strike-overs and the punctuation was rotten. Suppose you check up and make sure that both the scenario and the letter were written on the same typewriter."

"You mean two different people wrote them, but on the same machine?"

"Yes. It fits in with the theory of murder. By checking up on that typing we can find out a little more about it. Now, Rex, we should be able to find out more about this man. How about labels in his clothes?"

"I'm checking on that. The coat was sold by a firm in San Francisco. There weren't any laundry marks on his clothes. But I'll check up on this other stuff, Doug, and let you know. Keep your head, son, and don't worry. We can handle it all right. G'by."

Selby hung up the telephone as Amorette Standish slipped in through the door and said in a low voice, "There's a man in the outer office who says he has to see you upon a matter of the greatest importance."

"Won't he see one of the deputies?"

"No."

"What's his name?"

"Carl Bittner."

Selby nodded slowly. "Show him in," he said.

Carl Bittner was filled with bustling efficiency as he entered the room. Almost as tall as Selby, he was some fifteen years older. His face was thin, almost to the point of being gaunt; high cheekbones and thin lips gave him a peculiarly lantern-jawed appearance.

"I'm Bittner," he said. "I'm with *The Blade*. I'm working on this murder case. What have you to say about it?"

"Nothing," Selby said.

Bittner raised his eyebrows in surprise. "I've been working on some of the large dailies in Los Angeles," he said. "Down there the district attorney co-operates with us and gives us any information he has."

"It's too bad you left there, then," Selby said.

"The idea is," Bittner went on, "that newspaper publicity will frequently clear up unexplained circumstances. Therefore, the district attorney feels it's good business to co-operate with the newspapers."

"I'm glad he does."

"Don't you feel that way?"

"No."

"There's some chance we could identify the body, if you'd tell us everything you know."

"Just what information did you want?"

"Everything you know," Bittner said, dropping into a chair, lighting a cigarette and making himself thoroughly at ease.

"So far," Selby said, "I have no information which would enable me to identify the dead man."

"Don't know anything about him, eh?"

"Virtually not a thing."

"Wasn't he mixed up with some Hollywood picture actress?"

"Was he?"

"I'm asking you."

"And I'm asking you."

"Don't some of your investigations lead you to believe there's a picture actress mixed up in the case?"

"I can't very well answer that question."

"Why?"

"As yet I haven't correlated the various facts."

"When do you expect to correlate them?"

"I don't know."

Bittner got to his feet, twisted his long mouth into a grin and said, "Thank you very much, Mr. Selby. *The Blade* will be on the street in about two hours. I'll just about have time to get your antagonistic attitude written up against the deadline. Call me whenever you have anything new. Good-by."

He slammed the door of Selby's office triumphantly, as though he had succeeded in getting the district attorney to say exactly what he wanted said.

8

Selby switched on the lights in his office and read the terse telegram he had received from the chief of police at Millbank, Nevada: "BROWER HAD MANY FRIENDS AMONG MINISTERS IMPOSSIBLE IDENTIFY FRIEND MENTIONED FROM DESCRIPTION."

Selby consulted his wristwatch. Shirley Arden and Trask should arrive to keep their appointment within fifteen minutes.

Selby spread out *The Blade* on his desk. Big headlines screamed across the front page: "SHERIFF AND DISTRICT ATTORNEY BAFFLED BY CRIME. NEW AND INCOMPETENT OFFICIALS ADMIT HELPLESSNESS—REFUSE AID OF PRESS—UNIDENTIFIED CLERGYMAN MURDERED IN DOWNTOWN HOTEL!"

There followed a more or less garbled account of the crime, but that which made Selby's jaw clinch was a column of "Comment" under the by-line of Carl Bittner, written with the technique of a mud-slinging metropolitan newspaper reporter.

"When the district attorney, Selby, was interviewed at

64

a late hour this afternoon," the article stated, "he admitted he had no information whatever which would be of any value in solving the murder. This, in spite of the fact representatives of *The Blade* have been able to uncover several significant facts which will probably clear up the mystery, at least as to the identity of the murdered man.

"For some time a rumor has been rife that a prominent Hollywood picture actress figures in the case, that for reasons best known to himself District Attorney Selby is endeavoring to shield this actress. Pressed for information upon this point, Selby flew into a rage and refused to answer any questions. When it was pointed out to him that an identification of the victim, perhaps a solution of the crime itself, depended upon enlisting the aid of the press, he obstinately refused to divulge any information whatever, despite his admission that he was groping entirely in the dark.

"It is, of course, well known that whenever the breath of scandal fastens itself upon any prominent actress great pressure is brought to bear upon all concerned to hush matters up. *The Blade* has, however, pledged itself to discover the facts and give the news to its readers. It is to be regretted that the district attorney cannot recognize he is not a ruler but a public servant. He is employed by the taxpayers, paid from tax monies, and has taken an oath to faithfully discharge the duties of his office. He is young, untried and, in matters of this sort, inexperienced. Citizens of this community may well anticipate a carnival of crime as the crooks realize the type of man who has charge of law enforcement.

"During the campaign, Selby was ready enough with

his criticisms of Roper's methods of conducting the office; but now that he has tried to take over the reins, his groping, bewildered attempts to solve a case which Roper would have taken in his stride, show only too well the cost to the public of discharging a faithful and efficient servant merely because of the rantings of some youth whose only qualification for the position is that he wants the prestige which goes with the title."

Another editorial, on the editorial page, dealt with the fact that, as had been predicted by *The Blade*, Rex Brandon and Douglas Selby, while they were perhaps well-meaning, were utterly incompetent to handle a murder case such as the mysterious death of the unidentified clergyman. Had the voters retained Sam Roper in office, the editorial said, there was little doubt but what that veteran prosecutor would have by this time learned the identity of the dead man and probably had the murderer behind bars. Certainly the community would have been spared the humiliation of having a sheriff and district attorney engage in such a comedy of errors as had resulted in bringing to an unfortunate woman the false information that her husband was dead. Roper would undoubtedly have made an investigation before jumping at such a false and erroneous conclusion.

Selby squared his shoulders.

All right, they wanted to fight, did they? Very well, he'd fight it out with them.

He heard a knock on his door and called, "Come in."

The door opened and Selby saw a man nearly six feet tall, weighing well over two hundred pounds, smiling at him from the doorway.

The visitor wore a checked coat. His well-manicured hands adjusted the knot of his scarf as he smiled and said, in a deep, dramatic voice, "Ah, Mr. Selby, I believe? It is a pleasure."

"You're Trask?" Selby asked.

The big man bowed and smiled.

"Come in," Selby said, "and tell Miss Arden to come in."

"Miss Arden . . . er . . . er . . . unfortunately is not able to be present, Mr. Selby. As you may or may not know, Miss Arden's nerves have been bothering her somewhat of late. She has been working under a terrific strain and . . ."

"Where is she?" Selby interrupted, getting to his feet.

"At the close of the shooting this afternoon," Trask said, "Miss Arden was in an exceedingly nervous condition. Her personal physician advised her . . ."

"Where is she?"

"She . . . er . . . went away."

"Where?"

"To the seclusion of a mountain resort where she can get a change in elevation and scenery and complete rest."

"Where?"

"I am afraid I am not at liberty to divulge her *exact* location. The orders of her physician were most explicit."

"Who's her physician?"

"Dr. Edward Cartwright."

Selby scooped up the telephone. "You come in and sit down," he said to Trask, and, into the telephone, "This is Douglas Selby, the district attorney, speaking. I want to talk with Dr. Edward Cartwright in Los Angeles. I'll hold the wire."

Standing with his feet spread apart, his jaw thrust forward, the receiver of the telephone held in his left hand, he said to Trask, "That's what I get for giving a heel like you a chance to double-cross me. It won't happen again."

Trask strode toward him, his eyes glowering with indignation. "Are you referring to me?" he demanded in a loud, booming voice. "Are you calling me a heel? Are you intimating that I double-crossed you because Miss Arden's health has been jeopardized by overwork?"

"You're damned right I am," Selby said. "I'll tell you more about it when I've talked with this doctor on the telephone."

Into the telephone he said, "Hello . . . rush through that call."

A woman's voice said, "Dr. Cartwright's residence."

Selby listened while the long distance operator said, "The district attorney's office at Madison City is calling Dr. Cartwright."

"I'm afraid Dr. Cartwright can't come to the telephone," the woman's voice said.

Selby interrupted. "I'll talk with whoever's on the phone," he said.

"Very well," the operator told him.

"Who is this?" Selby asked.

"This is Mrs. Cartwright."

"All right," Selby said, "this is Douglas Selby. I'm the district attorney at Madison City. You put Dr. Cartwright on the telephone."

"But Dr. Cartwright has given orders that he is not to be disturbed."

"You tell Dr. Cartwright he can either talk on the telephone or I'll have him brought up here and he can do his talking in front of a grand jury."

"But . . . you couldn't do that," the woman protested.

"That," Selby remarked, "is a matter of opinion. Please convey my message to Dr. Cartwright."

"He's very tired. He left orders that . . ."

"Convey that message to Dr. Cartwright," Selby said, "or I'll get a statement from him which will be made at *my* convenience rather than at *his*."

There was a moment's pause and the woman's voice said dubiously, "Very well, just hold the phone a moment."

Trask interrupted to say, "You can't do this, Selby. You're getting off on the wrong foot. Now I want to be friendly with you."

"You," Selby told him, "shut up. You promised me to have Shirley Arden here at eight o'clock. I'm already being put on the pan for falling for this Hollywood hooey. I don't propose to be made the goat."

"If you're going to be nasty about it," Trask said with an air of injured dignity, "it happens that *I* know my *legal* rights in the premises and . . ."

A man's voice said, "Hello," on the telephone, and Selby said, "Shut up, Trask. . . . Hello. . . . Is this Dr. Cartwright?"

"Yes."

"You're the Dr. Cartwright who attends Shirley Arden, the picture actress?"

"I have attended her on occasion, yes."

"When did you last see her?"

"What's the object of this inquiry?"

"Miss Arden was to have been in my office this evening. She isn't here. I want to know why."

"Miss Arden was in an exceedingly nervous condition."

"When did you see her?"

"This afternoon."

"What time?"

"About three o'clock."

"What did you tell her?"

Dr. Cartwright's voice became very professional. "I found that her pulse was irregular, that her blood pressure was higher than should have been the case. There was some evidence of halitosis, indicating a nervous indigestion. She complained of migraine and general lassitude. I advised a complete rest."

"Did you advise her specifically not to keep her appointment with me?"

"I advised her not to engage in any activity which would cause undue excitement or nervousness."

"Did you advise her not to keep her appointment with me?"

"I advised her to seek a secluded mountain resort where she could be quiet for a few days."

"Did you advise her not to keep her appointment with me?"

"I told her that it would be unwise for her to . . ."

"Never mind that," Selby said, "did you tell her not to keep her appointment with me?"

"She asked me if it wouldn't be inadvisable for her to subject herself to a grueling interrogation after taking an automobile ride of some hundred miles, and I told her that it would."

"Specifically, what did you find wrong with her?"

"I'm afraid I can't discuss my patient's symptoms. A matter of professional privilege, you know, Mr. Selby. But I felt that her health would be benefited by a complete change of scenery."

"For how long?"

"Until she feels relief from some of the symptoms."

"And what are the symptoms?"

"General lassitude, nervousness, a severe migraine."

"What's migraine?" Selby asked.

"Well, er . . . a headache."

"In other words, she had a headache and said she didn't feel well, so you told her she didn't need to keep her appointment with me, is that right?"

"That's putting rather a blunt interpretation on it."

"I'm cutting out all of the verbal foolishness," Selby said, "and getting down to brass tacks. That's the effect of what you told her, isn't it?"

"Well, of course, it would have that effect and . . ."

"Thank you, Doctor," Selby said tersely, "you'll probably hear more from me about this."

He dropped the telephone receiver down between the prongs of the desk phone, turned to Trask and said, "The more I see of this, the less I like it."

Trask pulled down his waistcoat and became coldly dignified.

"Very well," he said, "if you're going to adopt that attitude, may I suggest, Mr. Selby, that in the elation of your campaign victory, you have, perhaps, emerged with a swollen concept of your own power and importance.

"As Miss Arden's manager, I have received advice from the very best legal talent in Los Angeles as to our rights in the matter.

"Frankly, I considered it an arbitrary and high-handed procedure when you telephoned and stated that Miss Arden, a star whose salary per week amounts to more than yours for a year, drop everything and journey to your office. However, since it is her duty as a citizen to co-operate with the authorities, I made no vehement protest.

"The situation was different when it appeared that Miss Arden's nerves were weakening under the strain and that her earning capacity might be impaired if she complied with your unwarranted demands upon her time. I therefore employed counsel and was advised that, while you have a right to have a subpoena issued for her, compelling her attendance before the grand jury, you have no right to order her to appear for questioning in your office. Incidentally, it *may* interest you to know that a subpoena, in order to be valid, has to be served in person upon the witness named in the subpoena. I think I need only call to your attention the fact that Miss Arden has virtually unlimited resources at her command, to point out to you how difficult it would be for you to serve such a subpoena upon her. Moreover, she is under no obligation to obey such a subpoena, if to do so would jeopardize her health. You are not a physician. Dr. Cartwright is. His diagnosis of the condition of Miss Arden is entitled to far more weight than your hasty assumption that her headaches and nervous fits are unimportant.

"I'm sorry to have to talk to you this way, but you asked for it. You're a district attorney in a rather unimportant, outlying county. If you think you can pick up your telephone and summon high-priced picture stars, who are of international importance, to your city, regardless of their own health or personal convenience, you're mistaken."

Trask thrust out his jaw belligerently and said, "Have I made myself clear, Mr. Selby?"

Doug Selby stood with his long legs spread apart, hands thrust deep in his trousers pockets. His eyes burned steadily into those of Trask.

"You're damned right you've made yourself clear," he said. "Now *I'll* make *myself* clear.

"I have reason to believe that Miss Arden was in this city, registered in the Madison Hotel under an assumed name. I have reason to believe that a man who was murdered in that hotel called on Miss Arden in her room. I have reason to believe that Miss Arden paid him a large sum of money. Now you can force me to use a subpoena. You may be able to keep me from serving that subpoena. But, by God, you can't keep me from giving the facts to the press.

"You're probably right in stating that Miss Arden's salary per week is greater than mine for a year, but when it comes to a show-down, the ability to dish it out and to take it isn't measured by salary contracts. I'm just as good a fighter as she is, just as good a fighter as you are—and probably a damned sight better.

"You've done a lot of talking about Miss Arden's importance, about the fact that she's an internationally known figure. You're right in that. That's the thing that gives you these resources you boast of, the money to hire bodyguards, to arrange for an isolated place of concealment where it would be hard to locate her with a subpoena.

"You overlook, however, that this very fact is also your greatest weakness. The minute the Associated Press and the United Press get the idea Miss Arden may be mixed up in this case, they'll have reporters pouring into town like flies coming to a honey jar. I didn't want to make any public announcement until I'd given Miss Arden a chance to explain. If she doesn't want to co-operate with me, that's her lookout."

Selby consulted his wristwatch. "It's twelve minutes past eight. I don't think Miss Arden's got to any part of the state where she can't get here within four hours' fast driving. I'll give you until midnight to produce her. If you don't produce her, I'll tell the press exactly why I want to talk with her."

Trask's face was a wooden mask, but his eyes showed a trace of panic.

"Young man," he said, "if you did that, you'd be sued for criminal libel and defamation of character, you . . ."

"You're wasting time talking," Selby said. "If you're going to get Miss Arden here by midnight, you'd better get started."

Trask took a deep breath, forced a smile to his face, came toward Selby.

"Now, listen, Mr. Selby," he said in a conciliatory tone, "perhaps I *was* a little hasty. After all, you know, our nerves get worn thin in this picture business. Miss Arden's trip to Madison City was highly confidential, but since you're interested in it, I think I can explain to you just why she came and . . ."

"I don't want your explanation," Selby interruped coldly, "I want hers."

Trask's face flushed. "You mean you refuse to listen to what I have to say?"

"At times," Selby said, "you're rather good at interpreting the English language."

Trask fumbled for a cigar in his waistcoat pocket.

"Surely," he said, "there's *some* way in which we can get together. After all . . ."

"I'll be available until midnight," Selby interrupted. "In the meantime, Mr. Trask, I don't think I need to detain you."

"That's final?" Trask asked, clamping his teeth down on the end of the cigar and giving it a vicious, wrenching motion with his wrist to tear off the end.

"That's final," Selby said.

Trask spat out the bit of tobacco as he reached for the doorknob.

"You'll sing a different tune when we get done with you!" he said, and slammed the door behind him.

Selby called Cushing at the Madison Hotel.

"Cushing," he said, "I want you to ask all of the regular roomers on the third floor if they heard any typewriting in three twenty-one on Monday night or Tuesday morning. It'll probably look better if you ask them."

Cushing said, "This is giving the hotel an awful black eye, Doug. That publicity in *The Blade* was bad—very bad."

"Perhaps if you'd kept your mouth shut," Selby said, "the publicity wouldn't be so bad."

"What do you mean?"

"Some of the information must have come from you."

"Impossible! I didn't give out any information."

"You talked to the chief of police," Selby said. "You know where he stands with *The Blade*."

"You mean the chief of police is double-crossing you?"

"I don't mean anything except that some of the information in the newspaper didn't come from the sheriff's office, and didn't come from mine. You can draw your own conclusions."

"But, he has the right to question me," Cushing said, "just the same as you have, Doug."

"All right, then, he's the one to complain to, not to me."

"But in your position, can't you hush the thing up?"

Selby laughed and said, "You can gather just how much chance I have of hushing things up by reading the editorial page in *The Blade*."

"Yes," Cushing said dubiously, "still . . . "

"Quit worrying about it," Selby told him, "and get busy and question your guests on the third floor."

"I don't like to question the guests."

"Perhaps," Selby suggested, "you'd prefer to have the sheriff do it."

"No, no, no, not that!"

"Then suppose you do it?"

Cushing sighed, said, "Very well," in a tone which contained a complete lack of enthusiasm, and hung up the receiver.

Selby had hardly put the receiver back into place when

the phone rang. He picked it up, said, "Hello," and heard a woman's voice, a voice which was rich, throaty, and intimately cordial.

"Is this Mr. Douglas Selby, the district attorney?"

"Yes."

"I'm Miss Myrtle Cummings, of Los Angeles, and I have some information which I think you should have. It's something in relation to the murder case which has been described in the evening newspaper."

"Can you give it to me over the telephone?" Selby asked.

"No."

"Well, I'll be here at my office until midnight," he said.

There was something hauntingly familiar about the woman's voice. "I'm sorry," she said, "but it's absolutely impossible for me to leave. For reasons which I'll explain when I see you, I'm confined to my room, but if you could come and see me some time within the next half hour, I think it would be very advantageous for you to do so."

"Where are you?"

"I'm in room five fifteen at the Madison Hotel. Do you suppose you could come to my room without attracting any attention?"

"I think so," he said slowly.

"Could you come right away?"

"I'm waiting for several rather important calls," he said.

"But I'm sure this is *most* important," she insisted.

"Very well," Selby told her, "I'll be over within ten minutes."

He dropped the receiver back into place, put on his overcoat and hat. He closed and locked the office door but left the light on, so that Rex Brandon would know he expected to return, in case the sheriff should call at the office. He parked his car a couple of blocks from the Madison Hotel.

It was one of those clear, cold nights with a dry wind blowing in from the desert. The stars blazed down with steady brilliance. The northeast wind was surgingly insistent. Selby buttoned his coat, pushed his hands into the deep side pockets and walked with long, swinging strides.

Luck was with him when he entered the hotel. Cushing was not in the lobby. The night clerk was busy with a patron. The elevator operator apparently saw nothing unusual in Selby's visit.

"Going up to campaign headquarters?" he said.

Selby nodded.

"Gee, that sure was something, having a murder case right here in the hotel, wasn't it?" the operator said, as he slid the door closed and started the elevator upward.

Again Selby nodded. "Know anything about it?"

"Just what I've heard around the hotel."

"What did you hear?"

"Nothing, except this guy took the room and was found dead. Cushing says it couldn't have been a murder. He says it was just a case of accidentally taking the wrong kind of dope and that *The Blade* is trying to make a big thing of it. *The Blade*'s had a reporter snooping around here."

"Chap by the name of Carl Bittner?" Selby asked.

"That's the one. He's got the boss sore at him. Cushing thought he was one of your men ... and there's things about the dump that Cushing don't want printed."

"What things?" Selby asked.

"Oh, lots of things," the boy said vaguely. "Take this guy, Trask, for one. Anyone would think he owned the joint. And there's a room on the fifth floor they never rent. A dame comes and goes on the freight elevator."

The elevator stopped at the fifth floor.

Selby handed the boy a half dollar. "Thanks for the information," he said. "I don't want to be interrupted. I came here because I wanted to get away from telephone calls and people who were trying to interview me. Do you suppose you could forget about taking me up here?"

"Sure," the bellboy said, grinning. "I can forget anything for four bits."

Selby nodded, waited until the cage had started downward before he made the turn in the corridor which took him toward the room at the end of the corridor which they had used as campaign headquarters. When he saw there was no one in the hallway, he tapped gently on the door of five fifteen.

"Come in," a woman's voice said.

Selby opened the door and stepped into the room.

He knew at once that Shirley Arden had arranged every detail of the meeting with the training which years as an actress had given her.

The door opened into a sitting room. Back of the sitting room was a bedroom. In the bedroom a rose-colored light shed a soft illumination which fell upon the actress's face in such a way that it turned the dark depths of her eyes into mysterious pools of romance.

She was attired in a tailored suit of pearl gray. Its simplicity was so severe that it served to center attention upon her face and figure. Had she been ten years older, she would have worn a gown so gorgeously designed that a woman looking at her would have said, "How wonderfully she's dressed," but with that pearl gray tailored outfit, men, looking at Shirley Arden, would only have said, "What a beautiful figure she has! How wonderful her eyes are!"

She was seated on the arm of an overstuffed chair, one gray-stockinged leg thrust out at such an angle that the curves caught the eye. Her lips were parted in a smile.

And yet, perhaps as a result of her Hollywood training, she overdid it.

Perfect actress that she was, she underestimated the intelligence of the man with whom she was dealing, so that the effect she strove for was lost. Had she remained seated on the arm of the chair just long enough to have given him a glimpse of her loveliness and then got to her feet to come toward him, he would have been impressed. But her very immobility warned him that the effect had been carefully and studiously planned.

"So," Selby said, kicking the door shut behind him, "you were here all the time."

She didn't move. Her face was held so that the lighting did not change by so much as a hair line of a shadow. It was as though she had been facing a battery of lights for a close-up.

"Yes," she said, "I was here. I didn't want to talk with you unless I *had* to. I'm afraid Ben Trask didn't handle the situation very diplomatically."

"He didn't," Selby said. "How about your nerves?"

"I really *am* very nervous."

"And," Selby said, "I suppose the idea was to send Ben Trask over to bluff me. If he'd reported success then you'd have actually gone into hiding."

"I didn't want to take any chances," she told him. "Can't you understand? Think what it means to me. Think of my position, my public, my earning capacity. Gossip is a fatal thing to a picture star. I couldn't afford to have it known I was questioned in connection with the case.

"Ben is a very strong man. He's always been able to dominate any situation he's tackled. He makes my contracts for me and it's an open secret they're the best contracts in Hollywood. Then he met you—and failed."

She waited for the full dramatic value of that statement to manifest itself. Then, with the slow, supple grace of a dancer, she straightened her leg, swung it slowly forward, came to the floor as lightly as thistle down and walked toward him to give him her hand.

"It's delightful, Mr. Selby," she said, "to find you so human."

His fingers barely touched hers. "It depends," he told her, "on what you mean by being human."

"I'm certain you'll listen to reason."

"I'll listen to the truth," he said, "if that's what you mean."

"After all, aren't they the same thing?"

"That depends," Selby said. "Sit down, I want to talk with you."

She smiled and said, "I know I'm in your city, Mr. Selby, under your jurisdiction, as it were, but please permit me to be the hostess and ask you to be seated."

She swept her hand in a gracious gesture of invitation toward the overstuffed chair beneath the floor lamp.

"No," Selby said, "thank you, I'll stand."

A slight frown of annoyance crossed her face, as though her plans were going astray.

Selby stood spread-legged, his overcoat unbuttoned and thrown back, his hands thrust deep into his trousers pockets, his eyes showing just a trace of sardonic humor beneath a grim determination.

"After all," he said, "I'm doing the questioning. So if anyone is going to sit in that chair beneath the illumination of that light, it's going to be you. *You're* the one who's being questioned."

She said defiantly, "Meaning, I suppose, that you think I'm afraid to let you study my facial expressions."

He shrugged his shoulders and said, "I'm not wasting time thinking about it. Your facial espressions are going to be studied whether you like it or not."

"Very well," she said, and dropped into the overstuffed chair, carefully adjusting the light so that it beat down upon her face. Her smile was the smile of one who bravely faces injustice, nor was there any narrowing of the eyelids as her lips parted. "Go ahead, Mr. District Attorney," she invited.

Selby stood staring at her steadily. "It happens," he said, "that I saw that same expression in *Love Life*. It was, I believe, the way you looked at your prospective father-in-law when he came to give you money never to see his boy again."

She lost her fixed smile. For a moment there was blazing defiance in her eyes. Then her face became as a wooden mask.

"After all," she said, "it's the same face. And it would

naturally hold the same expressions that you've seen in pictures."

"Well," he told her, "I'm not interested in your facial expressions. I'm interested in your answers to certain questions."

"Go ahead and ask the questions."

"You were here in the hotel Monday morning, were you not?"

"I was."

"In this room?"

"Yes."

"Why did you come here?"

"On a matter of business."

"What was the business?"

"I decline to answer that question. It's a confidential matter."

"With whom was your business to be transacted?"

"I also decline to answer that question."

"Have you seen photographs of the man who was found dead in room three twenty-one?"

"No."

Selby pulled a photograph from his pocket, strode toward her and thrust it out in front of him.

"Look at it," he said.

It was a moment before she lowered her eyes, as though schooling her face against showing any expression, then she glanced at the photograph, raised her eyes to his and nodded a slow, solemn nod.

"Know him?" Selby asked.

"I saw him."

"Where?"

"In the hotel."

"What part of the hotel?"

"In this room."

Selby sighed and said, "Now *that's* a lot better. When did you see him?"

"It was some time in the morning, shortly before ten o'clock, I think."

"What was he doing?"

"He was talking with me."

"What name did he give you? Was it the name under which he was registered, Charles Brower?"

She shook her head and said, "No, that wasn't the name."

"What name was it?"

She frowned thoughtfully for a moment or two and then said slowly, "No, I'm afraid I can't remember what the name was, but I know it wasn't Brower. It was something that sounded like Larry, or something of that sort. I think it had a 'Larry' in it."

"In the last name?"

"Yes."

"You're sure it wasn't the first name?"

"No, it was the last name. I don't think he told me his first name."

"Why did he happen to come into the room here?"

"He knocked on the door. I went to the door to see who it was."

"Had you ever seen him before?"

She hesitated once more for a moment, then very decisively shook her head and said, "No, I had never seen him before."

"But you let him in?"

"Yes."

"Are you accustomed to admitting strangers to your room?"

"I want you to understand my position, Mr. Selby. You're an educated man. You're different from the rabble. You can appreciate the position of an actress. I'm really not my own boss. I'm owned by my public. One must, of course, use discretion, but, if you could have seen this man when he was alive, you'd have realized how harmless he was. And yet, harmless isn't exactly the word I want. He was inoffensive, but it wasn't merely a passive futility, if you understand what I mean, it was . . . well, he seemed to be at peace with the world and to be non-combative."

"And so you let him in?"

"Yes."

"What reason did he give for knocking on the door?"

"He said that he'd seen me come in, that despite my attempt to avoid recognition he had realized who I was. He'd seen me get out of the automobile in front of the hotel and followed me to the freight elevator. In some way he'd discovered that I was in this room."

"How long was it after you'd taken the room that he knocked on the door?"

"Less than half an hour. Perhaps fifteen minutes."

"If he'd seen you in the elevator, why didn't he knock immediately?"

"He told me that he realized it was an intrusion upon my privacy. He'd been trying to make up his mind to do it for several minutes. He said he'd stood outside of the door for several minutes before he knocked."

"What time was this?"

"As nearly as I can place it, about a quarter to ten."

"What did he want?"

"It was pathetic," she said. "He wanted me to do a certain type of play which he said would be of great benefit to many people. He was so earnest that I couldn't refuse to give him an audience. He said that he'd been one of my ardent admirers ever since I'd appeared on the screen. He'd seen me in every part I played."

"Go on," Selby said.

"He had a script which he'd written. He said that he'd been intending to come to Hollywood to present it to me personally."

"Do you remember the title of this script?"

"Yes."

"What was it?"

"It was titled, *Lest Ye Be Judged*."

"Did you read it?"

"I glanced through it."

"Thoroughly?"

"No, just casually."

"Why didn't you read it thoroughly?"

"In the first place, I knew that it would be no use. In the second place, I could tell from almost the first glance that it was hopeless."

"Why was it hopeless?"

"The way it was written, the theme of it, everything about it."

"What was wrong with it?"

"In the first place, it was propaganda. It wasn't a play, it was a sermon. People go to churches to hear sermons; they go to theaters to be amused."

"Did he want to sell you this?"

"No, he wanted to give it to me. . . . Well, I don't know whether he would have put a price on it or not . . . You see, the conversation didn't get that far. He told me that he had consecrated his life to the service of humanity and he thought that this was a duty I owed to my fellow beings. The conversation was all on that plane, if you know what I mean."

"Yes," Selby told her, "I know what you mean."

"Well, he showed me this script and asked me if I wouldn't take it and use it as my next vehicle."

"What did you tell him?"

"I explained to him that I was under contract to the studio; that I had absolutely nothing to say about plays; that the studio selected such plays as they thought would make good vehicles for me. They did that through a purchasing department which specialized upon that very thing. They didn't allow me to even make suggestions, except minor suggestions at conferences where the continuity was being worked out."

"Then what happened?"

"He tried to argue with me for a little while but he soon realized that I was telling him the truth, that I had absolutely no power to select the plays in which I was to appear, that a recommendation from me would be virtually valueless."

"And what did you tell him to do?"

"I told him he would have to submit it to the Hollywood office."

"Did you tell him you thought the Hollywood office would turn thumbs down on it?"

"No. I didn't want to hurt his feelings. He was so earnest, so wrapped up in his play, it was really pathetic."

The face of the actress showed an expression of sympathy, her voice was vibrant with emotion.

Staring at her, Selby was gripped by conflicting emotions. He knew, on the one hand, that she was a skillful actress, fully capable of portraying any emotion she chose; on the other hand, he realized that it would be exceedingly difficult for anyone who was fabricating what had happened at that interview to simulate such an emotion. Her manner radiated complete sincerity and that warm, rich sympathy which a broad-minded woman of the world would have held for the pathetic little person who had brought his hopeless scenario to her.

Moreover, everything she had said tallied with the facts as Selby knew them. He hesitated a moment, then said, "That's a very beautiful purse you have, Miss Arden."

"Yes, isn't it?" she exclaimed at once. "It was given to me by the director who handled my last picture. I'm proud of it."

"Do you mind if I look at it?"

"Not at all."

She handed it over to Selby, who studied it, apparently lost in admiration for its beauty.

"How does it open?" he asked.

"This catch," she said, "on top." She snapped open the catch.

Selby peered inside, saw a roll of bills, lipstick, coin purse, handkerchief and compact.

"If you don't consider I'm taking too much of a liberty," he said, and before she could stop him, pulled out the handkerchief. He could hear her gasp as he raised the handkerchief to his nostrils.

Selby couldn't tell the brand of perfume, but he did have a sufficiently discriminating sense of smell to know that this perfume was entirely different from that which had scented the five one-thousand-dollar bills which had been found in the envelope the dead man had left in the hotel office.

"What's the matter?" she asked with cold enmity. "Were you looking for something?"

"I was," he told her, "interested in perfumes. I think that perfumes are indicative of personality."

"I'm *so* glad you feel free to be perfectly informal," she said sarcastically.

There was an awkward silence as he restored the handkerchief to her purse and handed it back to her.

"Was there," she asked at length, "anything else I could tell you about the man?"

"I don't know. Is there?"

"Not that I can think of."

"Did he tell you where he was from?"

"Some little town in the northern part of the state, I think, but I can't remember that."

Selby stiffened to attention and said, "You mean in Nevada?"

She raised her eyebrows, then shook her head and said quite definitely, "No, it wasn't in Nevada, I'm certain of that. Some little town in California."

"And you can't remember the name of the place?"

"No, it was in northern California somewhere, a Riveredale, or something like that."

"Riverview?" he asked.

She shook her head and said, "No, that wasn't it, but there was a river in it, I think."

"Your memory seems to be rather faulty, doesn't it?"

Her laugh was throaty and musical. "The first time a fan stopped me to tell me how much he enjoyed my acting and asked for my autograph, I could tell you everything about him, what he had on, what he looked like, where he came from and all about him.

"Gradually I came to accept it as a part of the profession and now . . . Well, I won't say that I'm bored, because one is never bored by expressions of appreciation from the public, but put yourself in my position. I'm called on to use every ounce of my energy in keeping fit, in acting, in being spontaneous and vivacious whenever I'm seen in public. I have to remember literally hundreds of newspaper men, cameramen, directors, supervisors, film executives and agents. Then there are quite a few people I meet whom I never expect to see again. They're like . . . like telegraph poles whizzing by when you're traveling on a Pullman train, if you know what I mean."

"I see," he said.

"They tell me things about themselves and I smile at them sympathetically and work my eyes; but all the time I'm thinking about my last income tax return, how long I'm apt to be working on this present picture, whether the director is going to listen to what I have to say about the way I should say 'Farewell' to my lover in the picture, or whether he's going to insist on doing it according to some standards which don't register with me.

"I give the fan my autograph and turn loose my best smile on him. I know I'm never going to see him again and he's in sort of a daze anyway, dazzled by the mental concept of celebrity which he's conjured up to wrap around me as an aura."

Selby watched her narrowly and said, "You have rather a neat trick of turning phrases."

"Have I?" she asked, smiling dazzlingly. "Oh, thank you so much."

"I presume now," he told her grimly, "if I'd only ask for your autograph the interview would be complete, and I could pass out of your life with the mental classification of a human telegraph pole whizzing by your Pullman car."

She pouted and said, "Don't say that."

"Isn't it true?"

"Certainly not."

"Why not?"

She lowered her eyes and said slowly, "I don't think any woman who ever came in contact with your powerful personality would readily forget you."

"Our contact," he said dryly, "has been rather remote and somewhat difficult to obtain."

"Which," she countered swiftly, raising her eyes to his, "is the main reason I will never forget it. Ben Trask is a wonder when it comes to working things. He's good at diplomacy and at fighting. He can be either high-hat, belligerent, or very suave. He turned loose everything he had on you and it never even dented your armor. When Trask came back and told me that I had to submit to questioning, he was licked. The man was all washed up. I was literally thunderstruck. It's the only time I've ever known him to make a complete and ignominious failure. I'd have remembered you even if I'd never seen you. And this has been far from a pleasant experience, you know."

"The meeting with me?" he asked, eyes studying hers.

"Not that," she said, smiling, "you know I didn't mean it that way. I meant the worry and the anxiety."

"Why the worry, if you merely met this man in such a casual manner?"

"Because," she said, "he was killed. That was a shock to me. Whenever you talk with anyone and then learn of his death, you're shocked. And, I may as well confess, there was a purely selfish reason. Competition is so keen among the stars that we must have a one hundred percent potential audience in order to get by. In other words, it takes all sorts of people to make a world. There are reformers, crusaders, fundamentalists, profligates, intellectual people, and dumbbells. Whenever we do anything which antagonizes any one particular class, we narrow our potential audience by just that much.

"For that reason, no matter how great a star's success may be, she never dares to let people get to gossiping about her. Moreover, because, in the past, scandals have been hushed up by the use of money and influence, whenever an actress's name is connected with anything out of the ordinary, the public always feels that the real facts were hushed up. No matter how complete the subsequent vindication may be, there are always the 'wise' ones who will smirk and wink to show that *they* weren't fooled any.

"If my name is connected with that of a murdered man,

the big majority of newspaper readers would always re-member the one item of gossip and entirely discount every-thing that might be said by way of explanation. People all over the country would glance at each other across the dinner tables and say, 'Well, I see Shirley Arden's company managed to quash the investigation on the Madison City murder all right. I wonder how much it cost them?' "

Selby said slowly, "I see."

"So," she said, laughing, "you can understand my at-titude and something of my anxiety."

Selby nodded. "Well," he said, "I guess that about covers everything."

She got to her feet, gave him her hand and said, "Will you believe me when I say that it was a *real* pleasure to have met you, Mr. Selby?"

"Thank you," he said. "And, by the way, where did you get the five one-thousand-dollar bills which you gave this minister?"

He was watching her as a hawk watches a moving clump of grass in front of a rabbit burrow. Coming as it did, his question took her by surprise. He saw her shoulders heave as she gave a quick gasp, but her face didn't change its expression by so much as the twitching of a muscle. She raised gravely questioning eyes to his and said in a low, level voice, "Five one-thousand-dollar bills? Surely, Mr. Selby, you're making some mistake."

"I don't think I am," he told her. "I think you gave this man five one-thousand-dollar bills."

"Oh, but I didn't."

"You didn't?"

"Why, *of course not*! Why, whatever put any such idea as that into your head?"

"I had an idea that you might have done so."

"Why, he was just a poor country minister. I'll venture to say he's working on a salary of less than a hundred dollars a month, and probably gets that paid partially in produce. That coat he was wearing was shiny, and worn quite thin at the elbows. Everything about him spoke of the pinch of insufficient finances. His collar was frayed, his shoes had been half-soled at least once, perhaps twice. His shirt had been mended around the neck, his tie was all frazzled at the edges."

"You seem to remember a lot about him," Selby said thoughtfully, "for one who has forgotten so much."

She laughed and said, "Once more I must ask you to indulge in consideration for my psychological processes, Mr. Selby. Men who tell me how much they admire my acting are quite numerous, but it's not very often one comes in contact with a man who's so completely genuine, so whole-heartedly sincere as this man. Naturally, as a woman, I noticed his clothes."

"And you didn't give him any money?"

"Why, certainly *not*. Good heavens, if you had only read that scenario."

"I did read it," he told her.

She laughed and said, "Well, *that's* the answer to your question."

Selby said slowly, "I may want to question you again. I'm not going to bother you to come up here, but I may come to see you. Where can I find you?"

"You can get me on the lot. Simply ask for Mr. Trask."

"And get another run-around?" he asked.

She laughed and said, "Not from Ben. He knows when he's licked."

"And you'll be where I can reach you through the studio?"

"At any time. I'll leave word with the operator to connect you with Mr. Trask and Benny will see that you get in touch with me. . . . In fact, I'd really like to. You know, in our world of make-believe it's not often one comes in contact with a personality which has no pretense."

His eyes showed the question in his mind.

"You see," she said, rushing into swift speech, "it isn't that we're four-flushers so much as we're actors and actresses, and we deal in worlds of acting. Simulating emotion becomes easy. Therefore, frequently one finds it easier to pretend surprise or regret or interest, or perhaps anger, than to solve the situation by some other method. One unconsciously uses one's natural weapons, just as a deer escapes danger by flight and a porcupine by thrusting out its quills."

He laughed and said, "Well, Miss Philosopher, do you classify me as a deer or a porcupine?"

"As a very prickly porcupine," she said. "When your quills are out, Mr. Selby, you're exceedingly difficult to deal with."

"Well," he told her, "I'll try and be more tractable in the future."

"And if you're in Hollywood, you will give me a ring?"

"If anything else turns up about which I want to question you, yes."

"And must if be an official visit?"

"Surely," he said, puzzled, "you didn't mean otherwise?"

"Why not? I told you that I meet so few men who have no pretense in their make-up that it's refreshing to meet someone who hits straight from the shoulder and never backs up."

"Aren't you depending a lot upon rather a hasty judgment of character?" he asked.

She laughed again and said, "If you could only have seen yourself standing with your legs spread apart, and your chin pushed forward! You looked like a man who expects to have a wade right through an avalanche and who is perfectly willing to do it."

"Perhaps *that*," he told her, "is just a pose."

"No," she said, "I know too much about poses. And you still haven't answered my question. *Must* it be an official visit?"

"It's rather unlikely that I'll be in Hollywood," he told her. "The duties of my office keep me chained down pretty well to this spot."

"Very well," she told him, with some indefinable expression in her dark eyes. "I won't press the point. I've never had a legal training, but I can tell when a witness is evading the question."

She was standing close to him now, and, as she raised her eyes, he felt drawn as toward some powerful magnet. It was as though he had been staring into an inky pool which had suddenly widened and risen toward him.

He laughed uneasily and said, "As though *you* ever had to give an invitation twice."

"Am I to take it that's an acceptance?" she asked.

He bowed low over her hand and said, "Yes. Good-night, Miss Arden."

"Good-night," she said, and her voice held a rich, throaty timbre.

He left the room, gently closed the door behind him, and took two or three deep breaths before the matter-of-fact environment of the familiar hotel corridor recalled him to the duties of his everyday existence.

He walked to the elevator, and was just about to press the button when he sensed surreptitious motion behind him. He flattened himself in a doorway and stared back down the corridor.

Carl Bittner had climbed up the stairs. In his right hand he held a camera and a battery photo-flashlight. Slowly, cautiously, he tiptoed his way down the corridor.

Selby waited until the reporter had rounded the bend in the hallway, then he rang for the elevator. In the lobby he paused to telephone room five fifteen.

"Be careful," he warned, when he heard Shirley Arden's voice on the wire, "a newspaper photographer is stalking the hallway."

"Thanks," she told him, "I've got my door locked."

"Has anyone knocked?" he asked.

"Not even a tap," she replied, "and thanks for calling."

Puzzled, Selby left the hotel to fight his way into the windy night.

9

Sylvia Martin was waiting in front of the locked door of Selby's office.

"Thought you were playing possum on me," she said. "I've been knocking on the door. I even tried a kick or two." And she glanced ruefully down at the toes of her shoes.

"No," Selby said, "I was out on what might be described as an emergency call."

"Anything new?" she asked.

He shook his head.

"Why is it," she asked, "that a friendly paper doesn't get any of the breaks while the opposition scores all the scoops?"

"Meaning *what*?"

"Meaning," she said, "that there's something going on at the Madison Hotel."

"What makes you think so?"

"A little bird told me."

"I'd like to know more about your little bird."

"If you must know, it's someone who advised me that Carl Bittner, the crack reporter whom *The Blade* has imported to scoop you on a solution of the murder case, received a mysterious telephone call and then went rushing over to the hotel, carrying a camera."

"Well?" he asked.

She said, "Let's go in and sit down where we can talk."

Selby unlocked the door. She followed him into his private office, perched on the edge of his desk, kicking one foot in a swinging circle.

"Come on," she said, "what's the low-down?"

"I'm sure I couldn't tell you."

"Have I got to wait until I read about it in *The Blade* tomorrow night?"

"*The Blade* won't publish anything about it."

"Don't ever think they won't. You're acting like an ostrich, Doug, sticking your head in the sand and kidding yourself you're hidden from view."

"I'm sorry," he said, "but there's nothing I could tell you, Sylvia."

"Why?"

"In the first place, what makes you think there's something to tell?"

"Don't kid me, Doug, I know there is. I suppose I can go over to the hotel and dig it out myself, if I have to, but it does seem to me that . . ."

She broke off the sentence but her foot swung more rapidly and in a wider arc until she seemed to be viciously kicking at the atmosphere.

Selby said, "I'd like to, Sylvia, I'd like to take you into my confidence, but you've got your job and I've got mine. You're representing a newspaper. It's your duty to gather publicity. Anything that you get will be spread on the front page of that paper. I have to take that into consideration."

"We supported you during the election. Don't we get anything in return for it?"

"Certainly you do. You get any of the breaks I can give you."

"A lot *that* means," she said bitterly. "The city editor put me on this murder case. I've known you for years. I've fought for you ever since you turned those damned twinkling blue eyes of yours on me and smiled. The newspaper I represent helped put you in office. What do we get in return for it? Not one damned thing!"

She blinked her eyes rapidly.

"Please don't cry, Sylvia," he begged. "You don't appreciate my position."

She jumped to her feet and said, "You make me so mad I *could* cry. Don't you see the position you're in? Don't you see the position that I'm in? Don't you see the position my paper's in?"

"I think I do."

"No, you don't. I've been assigned to cover the activities of the district attorney's office in connection with this murder case. I'm making a lamentable failure of it. The things I've found out could have been put in my city editor's eye without making him so much as blink. The opposition newspaper has imported a crack reporter. That means I'm being pitted against a trained investigator from one of the big metropolitan dailies. It's an opportunity for me to do something big. It's also an opportunity for me to become the laughingstock of everyone in the newspaper business. I need every advantage I can get. And about the only advantage I'm supposed to have is your friendship."

"Sylvia, I'm going to do everything I can for you, but . . ."

"That stuff makes me sick," she declared. "You know as well as I do that you're concealing something. You're good enough to conceal it from me because I'm fair enough to trust you; but you're not smart enough to conceal it from *The Blade* because they're fighting you and are out on their own, getting their information independently."

"What makes you think that they're going to get any particularly startling information?" he asked.

"Will you swear to me that your business at the Madison Hotel wasn't connected with some angle of this case?"

"No," he said frankly, "it was."

"And you saw someone there?"

"Naturally."

"Whom did you see?"

"I can't tell you."

"Why not?"

"Because I can't."

"Why?"

"It wouldn't be fair."

"To whom?"

He thought for a moment and then said lamely, "To the taxpayers, to the Prosecution's side of the case."

"Bosh!" she told him. "You're protecting someone. Who?"

"Suppose I should tell you," he said, "that some person

had become involved in this case who was entirely innocent of any connection with it except one brought about through casual coincidence? Suppose I should further tell you that the newspaper-reading public wouldn't believe that such was the case if it were given any publicity? Suppose, because of my official position, I'd been able to get a complete and frank statement of facts, given to me in a sacred confidence? Would you want me to betray that confidence to the first newspaper reporter who asked me?"

She shook her head impatiently and said, "Now I'll do some supposing. Suppose there's an angle to this case which is going to be given inevitable publicity? Suppose the story is going to be published in a hostile newspaper tomorrow night? Suppose we're going to be scooped on the thing. Don't you think it would be more fair for you to give me the news than to withhold it?"

"But you wouldn't want me to violate a confidence, would you?"

"Wouldn't it be better for the person who gave you that confidence to have the facts correctly reported in a newspaper which didn't deliberately try to distort them in order to belittle you?"

Selby was thinking that over when the telephone on his desk rang. He picked up the receiver and said, "Hello."

"Where the devil have you been?" Rex Brandon's voice rasped over the wire. "I've been trying to call you at intervals for the last twenty minutes."

"I took a quick run over to the Madison Hotel to investigate a development there."

"Find anything?"

"Nothing that I can discuss with you now. It's something we should talk over a little later. What have you got—anything?"

"Yes, I've got what may be a lead."

"What is it?"

"I've been talking with that oculist in San Fransico on the telephone. He's got a long list of names who have that same prescription, or correction, or whatever it is you call it. Among them are two ministers. One of them's a Reverend Hillyard from some little church in San Francisco, and the other's a Reverend William Larrabie from Riverbend, California."

Selby's voice betrayed his excitement, "Hold everything," he said. "That last name is the one we want."

"How do you know?"

"From some checking up I've been doing. I know that the man's name has the syllable 'Larry' in it and that he comes from a town in California that has a 'River' in its name."

"Okay," Brandon said. "What do we do next?"

"I'll tell you what we do," Selby exclaimed. "You hold the fort here. I'll rush to Los Angeles, charter a plane and go directly to this place. We won't take the chance of making a mistake this time, and we won't overlook any bets. I have a picture of the man with me."

"You don't think we should make the identification through the oculist?" the sheriff asked. "We could get a photograph up to him by plane within three or four hours."

"No, it's still a second-hand identification. Let's go right to the real source of information. I'm satisfied this is a hot lead. Remember, we've got a double problem. We not only have to identify the body, but we've got to find out why the man was here, what possible enemies he had, and what possible motivation might have led to his murder."

"All right," the sheriff said, "go to it. I'll keep running down leads here. Where can I reach you if I want to send you a wire?"

"Send the wire to John Smith at General Delivery, Riverbend," Selby said. "In that way, if any of the clerks in the telegraph office should be inclined to indulge in any gossip, we'll remove some of the temptation."

"When are you leaving?" Brandon asked.

"Right now," Selby said.

He hung up the telephone, turned to Sylvia Martin. "All right, sister," he said, "you claim you don't get any breaks. How would you like to go to Los Angeles with me and take a trip by airplane to identify this dead man? You'd be in time to wire an exclusive story to your paper."

She danced toward him, flung her arms around him.

"Doug, you *dear!*" she exclaimed, and left a smear of lipstick on his cheek.

"Of course," he said dubiously, dabbing at the lipstick with his handkerchief, "I don't know when I'll get back or just where we'll be. After all, there's the question of conventions . . ."

"The conventions," she told him, "be damned! Let's get started!"

10

The plane, a small cabin ship, roared on through the darkness. The altimeter registered an elevation of six thousand feet. The clock on the dash showed the time as two-fifteen.

A cluster of lights showed vaguely ahead, looking as glimmeringly indistinct as a gaseous nebula seen through a telescope. Directly below, a beacon light flashed warning blinks of red, then white, as a long beam from its searchlight circled the country like some questing finger.

The pilot leaned toward Doug Selby, placed his lips close to the district attorney's ear and shouted, "That's Sacramento. I'll land there. I won't take chances on a night landing farther up. You'll have to go on by car."

Selby nodded. "I've already arranged for the car," he yelled.

Her face looking wan from the strain and excitement, Sylvia Martin slumped back in the cushioned seat, her eyes closed, her senses fatigued by the steady roar of the motor which had beat a ceaseless pulsation upon her ear drums for more than two hours.

The lights of Sacramento speedily gained in brilliance, resolved themselves into myriad pin points of incandescence which winked and twinkled out of the darkness below.

The plane swung slightly to the right as the pilot got his bearings. The street lights came marching forward toward the plane in a steady procession. The pilot throttled down the motor, tilted the plane toward the ground.

As the steady pulsations gave way to a peculiar whining noise and the wind started to scream through the struts, Sylvia Martin woke up, smiled at Selby, leaned forward and shouted, "Where are we?"

The noise of the motor drowned out her words, but Selby guessed at her question, placed his lips close to her ear and yelled, "Sacramento."

The plane tilted forward at a sharper angle, the lights rose up to meet them. An airport showed below. The pilot straightened out and gunned the motor. With the roar of sound, flood-lights illuminated a landing runway. The pilot noted the direction of the wind from an illuminated wind sock, swung into position, once more cut down the motor and came gliding toward the ground. The wheels struck the smooth runway. The plane gave a quick series of jolts, then rolled forward toward the buildings.

As the plane came to a stop, a man wearing an overcoat and chauffeur's cap came walking out toward it. The pilot opened the cabin door. Selby climbed stiffly to the ground, assisted Sylvia Martin to alight. The slipstream from the idling motor caught her skirts, blew them tightly about the shapely limbs, then whipped them upward. She gave a startled scream, grabbed at her skirts, and Selby swung her clear of the wind current.

She laughed nervously and, forgetting for the moment there was no longer need to shout against the roar of the motor, yelled at the top of her voice, "I didn't know what to grab at first, my skirts or my hair."

The man in the overcoat and chauffeur's cap, coming up, heard her, smiled, tipped his cap and said, "Are you the parties who telephoned for the car—Mr. Selby?"

"Yes," Selby said, "I want to go to Riverbend. How long will it take us to get there?"

"Almost three hours."

Selby looked at his wristwatch and said, "All right, let's go. Can we get some coffee here?"

"Sure, there's a swell little restaurant where you can get almost anything you want."

They had coffee and hamburger sandwiches at the lunch counter. Sylvia grinned across at the district attorney and said, "Adventure, eh what?"

He nodded. His mood was as buoyant as her own. "Late hours for us country folk," he told her.

"You know, there's an exhilaration about riding in a plane," she said, sighing.

"Your first time?" he asked.

"Yes. I was frightened to death but I didn't want to say so."

"I thought so," he told her.

"That bumpy air over the mountains made me think the plane had lost a wing and we were falling."

"It *was* a bit rough for a minute. However, we're here now. It won't be long until we know the answer."

Her eyes sparkled over the rim of her coffee cup at him. "You know, Doug, I'm sorry I doubted you. It's a swell break to give me. I can telephone in a story that will be a peach . . . I suppose he's married . . . oh, I shouldn't be talking like this, but I'd be a hypocrite if I didn't. After all, he's dead and nothing I can do can call him back. Of course, I'm sorry that we'll have to be the ones to break the news to his wife and all of that, but I'm just enough of a news-hound to appreciate what a swell story it'll be. I can pack it full of human emotion. *The Blade* may or may not uncover something about the man's identity, but they can't get in on the ground floor, telling just how the news was received. They can't give an accurate word picture of the man's background, his home and . . . Oh, dear, Doug, you don't suppose there are kiddies, do you?"

"We don't know a thing in the world about it," he said. "We're not even definitely certain he's the man."

"Tell me, Doug, how did you know the name had a 'Larry' in it, and that he lived in a place that was a river something-or-other?"

He shook his head, looked at his wristwatch and said, "Finish up your sandwich. You can ask questions later."

She wolfed down the rest of the sandwich, washed it down with coffee, wiped her fingertips on the napkin, grinned and said, " 'Rotten manners,' says Emily Post, but 'Swell stuff,' says the city editor. Come on, Doug, let's go."

For several moments she was depressed, then, walking across toward the waiting automobile, she regained some measure of her spirits.

"Somehow," she said, "from the description we have of him, I don't think there are children. If there are, they'll be pretty well grown. Do you know what the population of Riverbend is, Doug?"

"I looked it up on the map. It's supposed to be three thousand two hundred, according to the last census."

"We'll get there," she said, "just about daylight. It'll be on a river, with willow trees growing along the banks. The place will look drab, just as dawn commences to break. There'll be a church which is in need of paint, a parsonage in back of the church, a poor little house trying to put up a brave front. . . . Tell me, Doug, why can't they incorporate religion?"

"What do you mean?" he asked.

"Fix it so that the big moneyed churches finance the little ones. You know as well as I do how hard it is to keep a minister going in a little town of three thousand people. There are probably four or five denominations represented in that town. Each one of them has its church and its minister."

"You mean they should consolidate?"

"No, no, not the denominations, Doug, but I mean the big churches should support the little ones. For instance, suppose this man is a Methodist, and say, in the big cities there are big prosperous Methodist churches. Why couldn't the big churches support the little ones?"

"Don't they?" he asked. "Isn't there an arrangement by which part of the man's salary is paid . . . ?"

"Oh, I don't mean that. I mean *really* support them. It seems a shame that the Methodists in Riverbend should support the Methodist Church in Riverbend, and the Methodists in San Francisco should support the Methodist churches in San Francisco. Why can't they all support churches everywhere?"

"You'll have to take it up with the churches," he told her. "Come on, get in."

She laughed and said, "I think I'm getting sentimental, Doug."

"You get over in that corner of the seat," he ordered, "and go to sleep. You're going to have a hard day."

She pouted and said, "My head will jolt around on that corner of the seat."

"Oh, all right," he told her, laughing, and sliding his arm about her shoulders, "come on over."

She gave a sigh, snuggled down against his shoulder, and was asleep before the car had purred along the smooth ribbon of cement highway for more than a mile.

She wakened as the car slowed, rubbed her eyes and looked about her. The first streaks of dawn were shrinking the beams of the headlights into little insignificant threads of illumination. The stars had receded until they were barely visible. The tang of dawn was in the air. The countryside was taking on a gray, spectral appearance.

A few scattered houses gave place to a street fairly well built up with unpretentious residences. The car slowed almost to a stop, turned a corner, and Sylvia exclaimed, "Oh, goody, the main street! Look at The Emporium, Doug."

"Where to?" the driver asked.

"I want to find the place where a Reverend Larrabie lived. I have a hunch he was a Methodist. Let's see if we can find the Methodist Church. Or we may find some service station that's open."

"There's one down the street," the driver said.

They drove into the service station. A young man, his hair slightly tousled, emerged from the warm interior into the chill tang of the morning air. He fought against a yawn while he tried to smile.

Selby laughed, rolled down the window and said, "We're looking for the Reverend Larrabie. Can you tell me where he lives?"

"Methodist Parsonage, straight on down the road two blocks, turn to the left one block," the young man said. "May I clean your windshield for you? And how's the water in your radiator?"

The driver laughed and said, "You win, Buddy, fill 'er up."

They waited while the car was being serviced, then once more started on. By this time the sky was showing a bluish tint. Birds were timidly throating the first tentative notes of a new dawn. They rounded the corner to the left and saw a small white church building which, even in the dim light of early dawn, showed that it was sadly in need of paint. As the driver slid the car in close to the curb and stopped it, a dog began to bark. Aside from that, there was no sign of life in the street.

"Well," the driver said, "here we are."

He opened the door. Selby stepped out, gave his hand to Sylvia. They crossed a strip of unpaved sidewalk, opened a gate in a picket fence. The dog across the street began to bark hysterically.

Sylvia was looking about her, her eyes alight with interest, her cheeks flushed.

"Perfect!" she exclaimed. "Absolutely priceless!"

They walked up a little graveled walk, their heels crunching the pebbles, sounding absurdly loud in the hush of early morning. Doug Selby led the way up the wooden steps to the porch, crossed to the door and rang the bell. A faint jangling sound could be heard from the interior of the house. The district attorney opened the screen door and pounded with his knuckles on the panels of the door.

"Oh, there *must* be someone home. There simply *has* to be," Sylvia said in a half whisper.

Once more Selby's knuckles beat a tattoo on the panels of the door. Sylvia Martin pressed a gloved thumb against the bell button.

From within the house came the sounds of muffled footsteps.

Sylvia, who had been holding her breath, started to breathe again and laughed nervously. "Doug," she said, "I'm so excited I could almost burst!"

The footsteps approached the door. The knob turned, the door opened. A motherly woman, with hair which had just commenced to turn gray and was tousled about her head, a bathrobe wrapped about her, what was evidently a flannel nightgown showing through the opening in the neck of the robe, surveyed them with patient gray eyes.

All of the elation fled from Sylvia's manner. "Oh, you poor thing," she said in a half whisper which was vibrant with sympathy.

"What is it?" the woman asked.

"I'm looking for the Reverend Larrabie."

The patient eyes surveyed them both, looked past them to the autombile which had pulled up against the curb.

"Eloping?" she asked.

Selby had known this was going to be difficult. He had hardly realized it was going to be quite so awkward.

"No," he said, "we're looking for the Reverend Larrabie."

"He isn't here. I don't expect him back for three or four days."

"Are you Mrs. Larrabie?"

"Yes."

"May we come in?" Selby asked.

She studied him with puzzled eyes and said, "What is it you want, young man?"

"I wanted to talk with you about your husband."

"What about him?"

"Have you," Selby asked, "a picture of him that I could see—some informal snapshot, perhaps?"

For a moment the eyes faltered, then they stared bravely at him.

"Has something happened to Will?" she asked.

"I think," Sylvia Martin said impulsively, "it would be a lot better, Mrs. Larrabie, if you could let us make certain before we talk with you. We could tell if we saw a photograph."

"Come in," the woman said.

Selby held the screen door open. Sylvia Martin slipped through and put her arm about the older woman's waist.

"Please don't worry, dear," she said, "there may be

nothing to it." Her lips were tightly held in a firm line as Mrs. Larrabie led the way into a front parlor, a room which was warm with the intimacies of living. A magazine lay face down on the table. Several periodicals were thrust into a magazine rack in the arm of a mission type chair, evidently the product of home carpentering. The shades were up and growing daylight furnished sufficient illumination so that they could see the interior of the room plainly.

The woman pointed to a framed picture. "That's he," she said simply.

Selby looked, and knew at once he had come to the end of his quest. The twinkling eyes of the apologetic little minister stared out from the photograph.

"May we sit down?" he asked. "I'm afraid we're bringing bad news for you, Mrs. Larrabie."

"What's happened?" she asked.

"Do you know where your husband is?" he inquired.

"I think he's in Hollywood."

"Do you know what he went there for?"

"No. What's happened?"

"I'm afraid that . . ."

"Sick?" she asked, in a calm, level voice.

"No," Selby said, ". . . not sick."

"Dead?"

Selby nodded.

Not a muscle of her face quivered. Her mouth didn't even twitch at the corners. But two tears welled into her motherly gray eyes, trickled unheeded down her cheeks.

"Tell me about it," she requested, still in that calm, steady voice.

"I'm the district attorney, of Madison City," Selby explained. "That's a city about sixty miles from Los Angeles."

"Yes, I know where it is."

"A minister came to the Madison Hotel and registered under the name of Charles Brower. He was found dead in his room. That was Tuesday morning. We've been trying to find out . . ."

"Why, *I* know Charles Brower," she said, her eyes widening. "If *that's* the one who's dead . . ."

"But it isn't," Selby explained, interrupting. "We thought that the man was Charles Brower because he registered as Charles Brower, of Millbank, Nevada."

"That's right, that's where Mr. Brower lives."

"We notified Millbank. Mrs. Brower came on and said that the body wasn't that of her husband."

"But it couldn't be Will. Will wouldn't register under an assumed name," she said with quiet conviction. "And he isn't in Madison City. He's in Hollywood."

"Do you know why he went to Hollywood?"

"I think he went there to sell a scenario."

Selby took the photograph of the dead man from his inner pocket.

"I'm very sorry, Mrs. Larrabie," he said, "but I'm afraid I'll have to disillusion you. Please prepare yourself for a shock."

He handed her the photograph. He noticed that her hand trembled as she took it. He saw her face grow gray.

This time her lips quivered.

"It's Will," she sobbed. "He's dead."

Selby gently took the photograph of the dead man from

her motionless fingers. Sylvia Martin knelt beside the other woman, her arm around the quivering shoulders.

"There, there, dear," she soothed, "you must be brave."

Mrs. Larrabie's toil-worn fingers explored the pocket of the bathrobe. Sylvia, divining her intention, opened her purse and took from it a handkerchief, with which she dried the tears in Mrs. Larrabie's eyes.

"Thank you, dear," the woman said, "you're very kind. Who are you?"

"I'm Sylvia Martin. I'm a newspaper reporter. Mr. Selby brought me with him. We're trying to find out who . . . who . . ."

Her voice trailed away into silence.

"Who what?" Mrs. Larrabie asked.

"The circumstances surrounding the death of your husband were very unusual," Selby said. "We're not entirely certain just what happened; but his death was directly due to an overdose of sleeping medicine . . . that is, what he thought was sleeping medicine."

"Sleeping medicine?" Mrs. Larrabie said. "Why, Will didn't take any sleeping medicine. He didn't need to."

"The circumstances," Selby insisted, "are exceedingly unusual. In fact, we think that death was neither natural or accidental."

"You mean," she asked, staring at him, her surprised incredulity for a moment overcoming the numbing effect of her grief, "Will was . . . murdered?"

"We're making a complete investigation," Selby said.

Mrs. Larrabie gave herself over to tears. She sobbed quietly into Sylvia Martin's handkerchief. Selby sucked in a quick breath, about to say something, but Sylvia flashed him a warning glance and shook her head. He remained silent, watching the crying woman with helpless sympathy.

Outside, the first rays of sunlight gilded the spire of the church, filtered down through the leaves of a tree to make a shimmering pattern on the glass of the window. Birds sang with full-throated vigor. The dog across the street burst into a paroxysm of barking, then was silent.

Mrs. Larrabie continued to sob into Sylvia Martin's handkerchief.

Finally she said, "We were so close to each other. We'd been childhood sweethearts. Will had the most lovable, the most whimsical disposition. . . . He had such a great faith in people. . . . He was always going out of his way to aid people. . . . Always looking for people in misfortune. . . . He visited the jails, always wanted to help the unfortunate. . . . That was going to cost him his position here. . . . Mrs. Bannister thought he wasn't devoting enough time to the members of the church. She was going to demand a change, and Will thought he could sell a scenario to the motion picture people and make enough money to devote all of his time to the unfortunate.

"He said the church members here were so smugly wrapped in their religion they didn't need any attention; that it was the poor unfortunates who really needed to be shown the way to God."

Selby said very gently, "I've got to ask a lot of questions about your husband's life. I must find out everything I can about the people with whom he came in contact, particularly about anyone who might have had any reason for wanting to harm him. Perhaps it would be better, Mrs. Larrabie, if you told us in your own way everything that you can."

She wiped her eyes, mechanically blew her nose on Sylvia's handkerchief, then suddenly said, apologetically, "Oh, you poor thing. I've ruined your handkerechief. Let me get you another and I'll send this one back to you all freshly laundered."

She got up from the chair and left the room.

Sylvia looked across at Selby, blinked her eyes and said, "Give me one of your h-h-h-hankerchiefs, D-D-Doug, I'm going to b-b-b-bawl, myself."

Selby came to her side, put his arm around her shoulders, gave her his handkerchief.

"I'm a h-h-hell of a reporter," she said, crying into the handkerchief. "I could have stood hysterics or wailing, but this quiet grief gets me. And right in the middle of it the poor thing had to think about my h-h-h-handkerchief. She's always thought about others all her life."

She wiped away the tears, smiled bravely up at Doug and said, "Isn't she a darling?"

He nodded.

They heard her steps in the corridor and Sylvia said, "Here, quick, take back your handkerchief."

Selby pocketed the handkerchief. Mrs. Larrabie returned to the room, carrying with her a handkerchief from which came the faint odor of lavender.

It evidently was one of her best, perhaps a Christmas or birthday gift. It was hand embroidered with the initial "L" in the corner.

"There, dear," she said, smiling, "you take that, and I'll be brave now. These things come to us. It's all part of God's plan. We aren't big enough to understand it. Death comes to everyone. It's part of His scheme of things."

"You said you knew Charles Brower?" Selby asked.

"Yes. I met him Saturday."

"When?"

"Saturday."

"You mean last Saturday?"

"Yes. My husband had met him at some of the conferences, and they were good friends. They'd worked together in Denver. My husband had a church there. That was years and years ago."

"How long ago?"

"Well, let me see . . . it must have been . . . about ten years ago."

"And your husband had kept in touch with Mr. Brower ever since?"

"Yes, they corresponded and met at conferences occasionally."

"And Mr. Brower was here Saturday?"

"Yes. That was the first time I'd met him."

"You're certain?"

"Why, my husband introduced him to me as Mr. Brower. He was here for dinner and said grace at the table."

"You have no children?"

"No, we had one baby, a girl that died when it was two days old."

"How did it happen that Mr. Brower came to visit your husband?"

"I don't know. They did quite a bit of talking. I think they'd been writing some letters."

"Where did Mr. Brower go when he left here?"

"Why, back to Millbank, I suppose."

"How did he come? Did he drive or come on the train?"

"He drove. He has a little car, rather dilapidated, but it gets over the road."

"And how did your husband go to Madison City?"

"I didn't know he went to Madison City."

"You knew he went to Los Angeles?"

"Yes, to Hollywood."

"How did he go?"

"On a bus, I think."

"He has a car?"

She shook her head and said, "No, we haven't needed one here. It's rather a small town. He can get around by walking."

"Did he have any hobbies?" Selby asked.

"Yes, helping people, hanging around the jails, and . . ."

"No, I mean any hobbies aside from that. How about photography? Was he interested in photography?"

For a moment her face underwent a change of expression. Then she said defiantly, "I think a man has to have some hobby in order to be normal. Will has been saving pennies for years. His camera gave him an outlet for his creative ability. He wrote a good deal and that helped, but he wanted to do something. He didn't have enough skill to paint, so he took up photography."

"And a very good thing he did," Selby agreed. "I certainly see no reason why he shouldn't."

"Well, Mrs. Bannister did," Mrs. Larrabie said. "She said it was positively sinful for a man to squander his meager salary on things which weren't necessary. She said that a man consecrated his life to God when he became a minister and that he should not have an ambition for worldly luxuries."

"She was referring to your husband's camera?"

"Yes."

"When did he buy it?"

"In December. We saved all our pennies—for years."

"Did he do his own developing work?"

She nodded. "He has a little dark room fixed up in the basement. Some of his pictures were beautiful. Of course, he didn't take many. The films aren't particularly expensive, but even so, we have to watch every cent, and Will was always patient about such things. He'd study the composition and the lighting on anything he was going to photograph for a long time before he'd use a film on it. He sent one of his prints to a photograph magazine and it was published with honorable mention. They said it showed rare skill in composition."

"What did Mrs. Bannister say to that?" Selby asked.

"She didn't know anything about it. . . . Oh, Mrs. Bannister is all right. I'm more bitter than I should be because she bothered Will so much. She simply couldn't understand his temperament and she didn't have enough patience to try, but she's a very wonderful woman, a wonderfully religious woman. If it weren't for her, the church couldn't stay here. She contributes almost as much as all the other members put together."

"And naturally wants to dominate the way the church is run?" Selby asked.

"She's very definite in her ideas," Mrs. Larrabie admitted.

"Had there been any open battle between her and your husband?"

"Oh, no, not at all. She isn't that kind. She sniffs and makes little remarks to other people. The remarks get back to us. But she doesn't come right out in the open and say anything directly. That isn't her way."

"How long have you been here in this church?"

"Five years."

"Has it been rather difficult for Mr. Larrabie—under the circumstances?"

"He's had his difficulties, yes, but everyone likes him. Of course, we've had to pinch and scrape on finances, but then, everyone does, and at that we're a lot better off than some of the poor people who lost everything they had in the depression. Our wants are simple and I think we get more out of life that way. We have time enough so we can be patient and Will had time to carry on his studies. We don't live at a rapid pace in Riverbend."

"How does it happen," Selby asked, "that your husband decided to go to Hollywood? With the limited finances at your command, it must have represented quite a cash outlay."

"That's something I can't tell you about," she said. "Will liked to be just a little mysterious about some of his business affairs. I thought perhaps he'd received an advance from one of the studios to come on and submit a scenario, or perhaps he'd sold something he'd written."

"And you don't know why he went to Madison City?"

"No, I didn't have any idea he was going to Madison City."

"And he had no enemies here in Riverbend?"

"Why, of course not. . . . Will didn't have an enemy in the world. He wasn't that kind."

"Could you show me where he worked?" Selby asked apologetically. "He had a study, I suppose? Was it in the church or . . . ?"

"No," she said, "it was right here. It opens off of this room. Here, I'll show you. He has the door locked, but I have a key."

She opened a drawer in the table, took out a key and unlocked a door which opened from the parlor into a little den.

There was a roll-top desk, a bookcase and a homemade vertical file. Everything about the room was scrupulously neat. There were no loose papers on the desk. On the walls were two enlarged photographs.

"Will took those," she said with pride, as Selby looked up at the photographs. "He enlarged them himself and made the frames."

Selby nodded and said slowly, "I want to go through his file of correspondence, Mrs. Larrabie. I'm very anxious to find carbon copies of some of the letters which your husband wrote before he made this trip."

"He never kept carbon copies of his letters."

"He didn't?"

"No. He did a lot of typing but I don't think he made carbon copies of anything. You see, it adds to the expense, and, really, there's no reason for it. Most of the stuff in that filing case is sermons he's written and notes on sermons, also stories. He wrote stories and scenarios. Not very many of them, but a few."

"Did he ever sell any?"

"No, they all came back."

Selby said slowly, "We're going back to Madison City, Mrs. Larrabie. I presume, under the circumstances, you'll want to go back to ... to take charge of things. I think perhaps it'll be necessary for you to answer some questions before the grand jury, and I'm going to give you a subpoena. It's just a formality, but it will enable you to get your traveling expenses."

When she made no answer, Selby turned from his survey of the room to look at her. Her tear-filled eyes were fastened upon the vacant chair in front of the roll-top desk. Apparently its full significance was just dawning on her.

The district attorney caught Sylvia's eyes and nodded. Together, they tiptoed from the room.

11

They returned to Madison City by train. As the rumbling Pullman clicked smoothly over the rails, nearing the familiar environs of the city, Sylvia Martin went forward to the vestibule, where Selby, standing braced against the motion of the car, was moodily regarding the scenery while he smoked a cigarette.

"Listen," Sylvia said, "I know the wife of a Methodist minister here quite well. Don't you think it would be a good plan, under the circumstances, to have her go there?"

Selby nodded.

"Why so pensive?" she asked him.

"I'm just thinking," Selby said, "that I may have overlooked a bet."

"How?"

"About that Brower angle. I should have made arrangements to locate him and have him subpoenaed as a witness. He knows more about this thing than we do."

"You think that he knew Larrabie was going to Madison City?"

"Of course he did. What's more, he must have known that Larrabie was going to register under his name."

"Why? What makes you think that?"

"Because Brower gave Larrabie his cards and his driving license."

"Unless Larrabie . . . No, he wouldn't have done that."

The district attorney smiled and said, "No, I would hardly gather that Larrabie was one who would knock his friend on the head with a club in order to get possession of an automobile which was probably worth less than fifty dollars."

"I wonder if they didn't come here together."

"Perhaps."

"But why?"

Selby shrugged his shoulders and said, "This is too deep for me, and I have a hunch it's going to be a humdinger—one of those everyday sort of cases where everything seems to be so confoundedly simple that all you have to do is to pick up the pieces and put them together. But when you pick up the pieces you find they just don't go together. None of them fit. It's like solving a jig-saw puzzle where you can't get any single piece to fit into any other piece. You've got no toe-hold, no starting point. Perhaps we've got the pieces of half a dozen separate jig-saw puzzles all scrambled together."

"Listen, Doug," she said, "I'm going to get horribly commercial."

"What do you mean?"

"I got a swell story out of that trip to Riverbend. The city editor is simply wild over it."

"Well?" he said.

"All those little touches," she said—"for instance, did you notice that the door on her house wasn't locked? She was staying there at night all alone, with her husband out of the city, but she didn't even lock the door. That's the kind of people they are and that's the kind of community Riverbend is."

He nodded and said, "But it isn't everyone who would have noticed that about the door not being locked, and not very many would have realized it's significance. It was a good story and you're entitled to the credit, Sylvia."

"You gave me the breaks."

He smiled down at her and patted her shoulder.

The train whistled for Madison City, started to slow to a stop.

"What I'm getting at," Sylvia said, "is that this is good for another story. I'd like to get an exclusive on it."

"Well?" he asked.

"Well," she said, "suppose you turn Mrs. Larrabie over to me?"

"Why?"

"I'd like to keep her where . . . well, to be frank, where reporters for *The Blade* couldn't get at her."

"How would she feel about that?"

"I don't know. I'm going to explain things to her and see how she feels about it. In that way I can get her living expenses paid. The paper would stand the expense."

Selby nodded slowly and said, "I can't give any official sanction to it, Sylvia. You'd better leave me standing here while you make your arrangements directly with Mrs. Larrabie. I've subpoened her to appear before the grand jury next week. I don't care what she does in the meantime."

She nodded, smiled and left him.

Selby finished his cigarette. The train ground slowly to a stop. The porter opened the vestibule door. Selby stepped to the platform, helped the two women to alight. Sylvia bent toward him and whispered, "It's all right. She understands, and she's grateful. She's going to stay with me. Suppose you go on to your office and leave us to shift for ourselves?"

"Very well," he said, "she has her subpoena. My duty's discharged when I've given her that. She'll want to see the body. There has, of course, been a post-mortem. You'd better prepare her for the shock of that. I'm going to my apartment and get a bath and get into some clean clothes. Also, I'll want to get in touch with Brandon and have a conference."

She grabbed his hand, gave his fingers a quick squeeze. "Thanks, Doug," she said.

He took a cab to his apartment, realized that he'd need to go to Los Angeles to retrieve the automobile he'd left at the airport. He felt a swift thrill of anticipation and realized that it was due to the fact he'd remembered his promise to Shirley Arden.

He turned hot water into his bathtub, telephoned the courthouse and asked for the sheriff. When he heard Rex Brandon's voice on the line he said, "Okay, Rex, we're back."

"You brought the woman with you?"

"Yes."

"Where is she?"

"Sylvia Martin has her in tow. Just between you and me, Sheriff, I think she's worked out some deal with her for exclusive story privileges."

"Okay by me," Brandon said. "*The Clarion* stuck up for us during the election. You didn't see last night's *Blade,* did you, Doug?"

"No."

"Better take a look at it. They've got a pretty good roast in there. What's this about the motion picture actress you're shielding having told you the man's name?"

Selby gripped the receiver so tightly that his knuckles ached.

"What's that? Something in *The Blade* about that?"

"Yes. They've put it up in rather a dirty way. They've intimated that you've been reached by money or influence, or both; that you're throwing up a big smoke screen to protect some prominent motion picture actress who's involved in the murder; that you met her at a secret conference and she told you who the murdered man really was. *The Blade* threatens to publish her name."

"Good God!" Selby said.

"Anything to it?" the sheriff asked.

"Yes, and no," Selby told him. "I'm protecting Miss Arden . . . that is, I simply didn't make her name public because I'm satisfied she had no connection with the case. I'd have told you about it if it hadn't been necessary for me to rush up to Riverbend to make that identification absolute."

"I was wondering," the sheriff said slowly, "how it

happened you were so certain that Larrabie of Riverbend was the man we wanted. You must have had a tip from somewhere."

"In a way, yes."

"Did it come from this actress?"

"Let's not talk about this thing over the telephone," Selby said. "Suppose you run out to my apartment? We can talk here."

"I'm just going to the Madison Hotel," the sheriff said. "I understand Cushing's found a guest who heard some typing across in three twenty-one. Suppose you make it snappy and meet me there?"

"I'm all grimy from travel," Selby said. "I'm just climbing into the bathtub, but I can make it in about fifteen or twenty minutes . . . only wait a minute, Rex, I haven't a car. I left mine down in Los Angeles."

"Suppose I drive around and pick you up?" the sheriff suggested.

"That'll be fine," Selby told him. "Be here in ten minutes."

He dropped the receiver back into place.

So *The Blade* knew about Shirley Arden, did they? And they'd turned the blast of dirty publicity on her. Damn them! He'd make them suffer for that. It was a dirty shame to drag her into it. That's what politics would do.

He stood there, eyes smoldering with rage, his fists clenched, his legs stretched far apart, and it wasn't until he heard the splash of water on the tiled floor of the bathroom that he suddenly realized he'd left the hot water running full force.

Selby flung bath towels on the floor to mop up the

surplus moisture, tubbed hastily and met Sheriff Brandon in exactly twelve minutes from the time of the telephone call.

"Listen," he said, "I'm getting fed up on this yellow journalism. I'm . . ."

"Take it easy, son," Rex Brandon advised, starting the car toward the Madison Hotel. "You've fought your way through a lot of stuff without losing your head. Don't begin now."

"It's the damned injustice of it," Selby said.

"Lots of things in the world are unjust, Doug."

"I can take it as far as I'm concerned," Doug Selby went on, "but when it comes to dragging in a woman, jeopardizing the career of an actress and perpetrating the dastardly libel by insinuation I get all fed up."

"The best way to win a fight," the sheriff remarked, "is never to get mad, and, if you must get mad, never let the other fellow know it. Now, get a smile on your face. We're going up and find out about that typewriting business. Maybe we'll run on to Bittner and maybe we won't. But, in any event, you're going to walk into that hotel smiling."

Selby took a deep breath, slowly his face twisted into a set grin.

"That ain't a smile," Rex Brandon said, "that's the sort of face a man makes when he's got a pain in his stomach. Relax a little bit . . . there, that's better."

He swung his car in to the curb in front of the hotel. Together, the two men entered the lobby.

George Cushing came toward them, his face twisted into a succession of grimaces. His head jerked with St.

Vitus-dance-like regularity toward the counter, where a man in a blue serge business suit was engaged in a low-voiced conversation with the clerk. On the counter in front of the man was a letter.

"Step right this way, gentlemen, if you're in search of rooms," Cushing said, and taking the surprised sheriff by the arm, led him over to the counter. He said to the clerk, "These two gentlemen are strangers in the city. They are looking for rooms."

The clerk looked up at Brandon and the district attorney. Recognition flooded his features, then gave place to a look of puzzled bewilderment.

"They're *strangers* in the city," Cushing repeated. "They want rooms. Go ahead and dispose of your business with this man."

The man in the blue suit was too engrossed in his own affairs to give any particular heed to the conversation.

"It's *my* money," he said, "and I'm entitled to it."

Cushing bustled importantly behind the counter and said, "What seems to be the trouble, Johnson?"

"This man says that he's entitled to an envelope containing five thousand dollars which Mr. Brower left on deposit in the safe."

Brandon moved up on one side of the man at the counter. Selby moved to the other side and nodded to Cushing.

"I'm the manager here," Cushing said. "What's your name?"

"You heard what I had to say a few minutes ago. You were standing over there by the safe. You heard the whole thing," the man said.

"I wasn't paying any particular attention to it." Cushing said. "I thought it was just some ordinary dispute. Mr. Brower is dead, you know. We can't hand over the money without some definite assurance that it's yours."

"I don't know what more you want than this letter," the man said. "You can see for yourself it says the money is mine."

Cushing picked up the typewritten letter, read it, then placed it back on the counter, turning it so that Selby and the sheriff could read it without difficulty.

The letter was addressed to George Claymore, at the Bentley Hotel in Los Angeles. It read:

"MY DEAR GEORGE:

"You'll be glad to learn that I've been successful in my mission. I have your five thousand dollars in the form of five one-thousand-dollar bills. Naturally I'd like to have you come up as soon as possible to get the money. I don't like to have that amount in my possession and, for obvious reasons, I can't bank it. I've given it to the clerk to put in the safe here at the hotel.

"I am signing this letter exactly the way I have signed my name on the envelope, so the clerk can compare the two signatures, if necessary.

"With kindest fraternal regards, and assuring you that this little incident has served to increase my faith and that I hope it will strengthen yours, I am,

"Sincerely,

"CHARLES BROWER, D.D."

Down below the signature in the lower left hand corner was typed "Room 321, Madison Hotel."

"Perhaps *I* can be of some assistance to you," Selby volunteered, "I happen to know something about Mr. Brower's death."

"You do?"

"Yes, in a general way. You're Claymore, are you?"

"Yes."

"And that, of course, is your money."

"You can read plainly enough what this letter says."

"You were in Los Angeles at the Bentley Hotel when you received this letter?"

"Yes."

"Let's see when it was mailed. It's post-marked from here on Tuesday. When did you get it?"

"I didn't get it until late last night."

"That's poor service," Selby said.

The other man nodded. There seemed about him a curious lack of self-assertion.

"I suppose," Selby said casually to Cushing, "the management here will want a brief statement of what the money was for and how it happened to be in the murdered man's possession."

He turned to the man at this side, smiled and said, "Go right ahead, Mr. Claymore, just give them a brief outline."

"Well," Claymore said, "it was like this. You see . . ."

He broke off, stared at the elevator, then turned abruptly toward the door.

"I'll be right back," he said.

Sheriff Brandon grabbed the man's coat tails, spun him around, flipped back his own coat lapel to show a gold-plated star.

"Buddy," he said, "you're back right now. What's the game?"

"Let me alone! Let me go! You've got no right to hold me! You . . ." He became abruptly silent, turned back toward the counter, stood with his shoulders hunched over, his head lowered.

Selby looked toward the elevator. Mrs. Charles Brower was marching sedately toward the street exit.

"She staying here?" he asked Cushing.

"Yes, temporarily. She's insisting that someone pay her expenses. She's hired Sam Roper."

Selby said to Brandon, "turn him around so he faces the lobby, Rex."

The sheriff spun the man around. He continued to keep his head lowered.

Selby raised his voice and called, "Why, good morning, Mrs. Brower."

The woman turned on her heel, stared at Selby, then, as recognition flooded her countenance, she bore down upon him with an ominous purpose.

"I've never been to law," she said, "but I've got some rights in this matter, Mr. Selby. I just wanted you to know that I've consulted a lawyer and . . ."

She broke off, to stare with wide, incredulous eyes.

"Charles!" she screamed. "What are *you* doing here?"

For a moment Selby thought that the man wasn't going to raise his head. Then he looked up at her with a sickly smile, and said, "As far as that's concerned, what are you doing here?"

"I came here to identify your body."

He wet his lips with his tongue, said in a burst of wild desperation, "Well, you see, I . . . I read in the paper I was dead, so I came here to see about it."

"What about this five thousand dollars?" Brandon asked.

The man whirled. The typewritten letter was still on the counter. His face held the expression of a drowning man, looking frantically about him, trying to find some straw at which he might clutch.

"What letter?" Mrs. Brower asked, moving curiously toward the counter.

Selby folded the letter and envelope and thrust it in his pocket. "This your husband?" he asked.

"Yes."

"Let's let him tell about it."

Brower clamped his lips together in a firm, straight line.

"Go on," Selby said, "I'd like to hear your story, Brower."

The man remained mute.

"Speak up, Charles! What's the matter with you?" Mrs. Brower snapped. "You haven't been doing something you're ashamed of, have you?"

Brower continued to remain silent.

"Go on, speak up," Mrs. Brower ordered.

There was something in the dominant eye of his wife which brought Brower out of his silence, to mumble, "I don't think I'd better say anything right now, dear. It might make trouble for everyone, if I did."

"Why, what's the matter with you? You jellyfish!" she

said. "Certainly you're going to speak up. Go right ahead and tell your story. You've got to tell it sooner or later and you might just as well tell it now."

Brower shook his head. Mrs. Brower looked at the men helplessly.

"Well, of all things!" she said.

"I'm afraid," Selby said, "that if you don't speak up, we're going to have to detain you for questioning, Mr. Brower."

A little crowd had collected in the lobby, and the interested spectators served as a magnet to draw more curiosity seekers.

The sheriff said quietly, "I think I'd better take him along with me, Doug. You stay here and look into that other angle. Then come on up to the jail. Perhaps he'll have changed his mind."

Selby nodded.

"Make way, folks," Brandon said cheerfully.

Mrs. Brower swung into step beside her husband and the sheriff. "Don't think you're going to take him where *I* can't talk to him," she said grimly. "He's got an explanation to make to me. . . . Out on a motor trip, huh? Resting his nerves, eh? The very idea! What sort of goings-on is that for a respectable married man, and a parson, at that."

Selby watched the crowd trail along uncertainly, saw the sheriff push his prisoner through the door and into the automobile, saw Mrs. Brower, with the calm finality of one who has implicit faith in herself and her ability to do anything she decides upon, climb into the rear seat of the automobile with her husband.

The sheriff started the car.

Selby caught Cushing's eye, jerked his head toward Cushing's office and said, "Let's have a little chat."

Selby followed the hotel man into the office and faced him.

"What about it?" the district attorney asked.

"This chap showed up out of a clear sky," Cushing said, "came walking up to the desk big as life, and asked if Mr. Brower was in his room. The clerk was flabbergasted. I was over by the safe. I pretended not to be taking any great interest in the conversation. The clerk told him, no, Mr. Brower wasn't in, and then the chap produced that letter and said Brower had left five thousand dollars in the safe for him. I signaled the clerk to stall him along, and I was just starting for the telephone booth to put in a call for you when you came walking in the door."

"You don't know anything more about him than that?"

"That's all."

Selby said, "Get out that envelope. Let's check the signatures."

"I haven't it. The sheriff took it up and locked it in his safe yesterday night."

"All right, I'll keep the letter," Selby said. "Now, I understand there was someone who heard typewriting in three twenty-one."

"Yes, a Miss Helen Marks."

"Where is she?"

"In her room."

"What's the number?"

"Three seventy-two."

"Have you talked with her?"

"Only generally."

"What's her story?"

"She heard typing in three twenty-one when she came in Monday night. She says it was some time around midnight."

"I think I'll talk with her," Selby said; "give her a ring and tell here I'm coming up."

"Listen," Cushing pleaded, "this thing keeps getting worse and worse. Guests are commencing to get frightened. Now, I'm entitled to some consideration from your office, Selby. I want you to catch that murderer."

Selby grinned and said, "Perhaps if you hadn't been so insistent that we hush it all up from the start, we might have got further."

"Well, that looked like the best thing to do then. You can understand my position. I'm running a hotel, and ..."

Selby clapped him on the back and said, "Okay, George, we'll do the best we can. What was that number, three seventy-two?"

"Right."

Selby took the elevator to the third floor and knocked on the door of three seventy-two. It was opened almost immediately by a dark-complexioned young woman in the early twenties. Her eyes were very large and smoke-gray. She wore a checked black and white tailored suit. Make-up showed bright patches of color on her cheeks. Her lips were smeared with lipstick until they were a glossy red.

"You're Mr. Selby," she asked, "the district attorney?"

"Yes."

"I'm Helen Marks. Come in. They said you were coming up to see me."

"You heard the typewriting in room three twenty-one?" Selby asked.

"Yes. It was Monday night."

"What do you do for a living? Do you work?"

"I'm not doing anything at present. I have been a secretary and a night club entertainer. I've clerked in a dry goods store and have done modeling work in Los Angeles."

"What time was it you heard the sounds of the typewriting?"

"I don't know. It was when I came in. Sometime around midnight, I would say, but that's just a guess."

"What had you been doing?"

"I'd been out with a boy-friend."

"Doing what?"

Resentment showed in her eyes. "Is that necessary?" she asked.

"Yes."

"We went to a picture show."

"Not until midnight."

"No, then we had some drinks and danced."

"Then what?"

"Then he drove me to the hotel."

"Straight to the hotel?"

"Yes, of course."

"Did he see you as far as the elevator?"

She frowned, and said, "Now, listen, I'm being a good sport and giving you the breaks in this thing. Don't ask so many questions."

"I'm sorry, Miss Marks, but it's necessary. You can rest assured that I'll keep anything you tell me in complete confidence, insofar as I can do so."

"Well, yes," she said, "he came to the elevator with me."

"Could this have been before midnight?"

"No, I'm sure it wasn't before midnight."

"It was probably after midnight, then?"

"Perhaps."

"How much after?"

"I don't know, I didn't look at my watch. I'm not accountable to anyone and I don't have to tell *anyone* just what time I came in."

"You heard this typewriting distinctly?"

"Yes."

"And remembered it?"

"Yes."

"Why didn't you say anything sooner?"

"I didn't think it was important."

"You've made a living by running a typewriter?"

"Yes."

"How did this typing sound to you? Was it the ragged touch of the hunt-and-peck system, or was it done by the touch system?"

"It was fast typing," she said. "I don't believe I could tell whether it was a touch system, but that typewriter was going like a machine gun."

"How long did you hear it?"

"Just while I was walking past the door."

Selby said casually, "And your boy-friend, I presume, can verify your statement?"

"Yes, certainly. . . . Why, what do you mean?"

Selby smiled at her.

"Well," she said, defiantly, "he came as far as my room."

"Did he stay?"

"He did not."

"Just went to the door of the room?"

"Well, he kissed me good-night."

"Once or more than once?"

"Listen," she said, "get this straight. This is the reason I didn't want to say anything about what I'd seen. I was afraid a lot of people would start asking questions that were none of their business. I'm straight. If I wasn't, it's no one's business except my own. The boy I was out with is a nice chap. I'll say that for him. He's a perfect gentleman and he knows how to treat a woman. He came as far as the room. He was here perhaps five minutes. He kissed me good-night, and—believe it or not—he was darn nice and sweet about it."

"And there's nothing else you can tell me—about the typing?"

"Not a thing."

"Can't you place that time a little more closely?" Selby asked.

"Well, it was after midnight. It might have been quite a bit after midnight."

"Don't you know that it was much later than that?" Selby said kindly. "After all, Miss Marks, I don't want to pillory you with a lot of questions, but this man died perhaps right around midnight. The question of time becomes important. Now can't you . . . ?"

"It was right around three o'clock in the morning," she said sullenly.

"That's better. Have you any way of fixing the time—definitely?"

"We danced until about a quarter to three. My boy-friend said he had to work in the morning and he couldn't make too big a night of it. So we came directly to the hotel."

"And went directly to this room?"

"Yes."

"And you don't think he was here more than five minutes?"

"No."

"You didn't go as far as the elevator with him when he left?"

"Of course not. He saw me to my room and that was all. When he left, I locked the door, took my clothes off and tumbled into bed. I was a little weary myself. It had been quite a night—you know, we'd been hoofing it."

Selby nodded.

"What's the name of your boy-friend?" he asked.

"Do you have to call him?"

"I'd like to talk with him."

"It's Herbert Perry," she said. "He's working at a service station in . . ."

Selby stiffened to electrified attention.

"Herbert F. Perry?" he asked. "The young man who's bringing a suit to determine heirship to the Perry Estate?"

She frowned for a moment and said, "I guess that's right. He said something about some lawsuit he was in. I gathered from the way he talked he didn't think he stood much chance of winning it. But he said if he *could* win it there's be a big bunch of money in it for him."

"And you don't know where he went after he left this room?"

"Why, he went down in the elevator, of course."

"But you didn't *see* him go."

"No, of course not."

"How long have you known Herbert Perry?"

"To tell you the truth," she said, "I just met him that night."

"Who introduced you?"

She stared defiantly at the district attorney and said, "It was a pick-up, if you want to know."

"On the street?"

"Certainly *not!* I stopped in at the bar at the *Blue Lion* for a drink. This boy was there. He was very nice. We got to talking."

"Did he," Selby asked, "seem to know anything about you?"

"What do you mean by that?"

"Did he know where you lived?"

"Come to think of it," she said, "he did say that he'd seen me a couple of times at the hotel and had inquired something about me. He knew my name. He said he'd been wanting to meet me for a week, but didn't know just how to arrange it. He was an awfully nice chap."

"So then you spent the evening together?"

"Yes, we hoofed around a bit and had a few drinks."

Selby smiled, and said as casually as possible, "Well,

thanks very much for coming forward with the information. Don't change your address without letting me know, because it may be important. It's rather difficult to believe that this man was alive and writing on his typewriter at that hour in the morning. . . . You don't think there's any possiblity you could be mistaken in the room?"

"No, because I noticed there was a light coming through the transom. I wondered who could be writing at that hour in the morning."

Selby smiled, thanked her again and sauntered casually out to the corridor. As soon as he heard the door close behind him, however, he raced for the elevator. In the lobby he crossed to the telephone booth, grabbed up the receiver and said to the operator in an excited voice, "Get me the sheriff's office, quick!"

12

Herbert Perry sat in the district attorney's office, facing the light. The sheriff and Douglas Selby concentrated upon him steady stares of silent accusation.

"Now, listen," he said, "this Marks girl is a nice kid, see? She's on the up-and-up. Of course, it was a pick-up, but that's the way things go nowadays. Times are different from what they used to be."

Selby said coldly, "I still can't see why you knocked on the door of three twenty-one."

"Well, that's what I'm trying to lead up to. She's a good kid. She wanted to sleep. I'd had a couple of drinks and I was feeling chivalrous. This typewriter was making a racket like a machine gun. The transom was open. You could hear the thing clacking all up and down the corridor. I figured it'd be a swell thing to tell this guy it was bedtime, see?"

Selby exchanged glances with the sheriff.

Perry twisted his neck around inside his collar, took a

deep breath and went on, "It was the thing anyone would do under the circumstances. The kid was trying to sleep. Lots of people in the hotel were trying to sleep. I'd had four or five drinks. I was feeling pretty good—not jingled, you understand, but mellow and protective—so I took the girl home and dated her up for a night next week. Then, when I started toward the elevator I felt kind of boyscoutish, so I tapped on the door."

"What happened?"

"The typewriter stopped."

"Did you knock again?"

"Yes."

"Get any answer?"

"No."

"Did you say anything?"

"No, not after he stopped typewriting. I figured there was no use doing anything else. . . . You know how it is, you're in a bedroom and you can hear some guy snoring in the other room. You knock on the wall. He rolls over and quits snoring. That's all there is to it."

Perry seemed pathetically eager to have them believe his explanation.

Selby tapped the top of his desk with an impressive forefinger and said, "Now, listen, Perry, you and I might just as well understand each other now as later. You knew this man in three twenty-one."

"*I* knew him?" Perry exclaimed, his eyes wide.

"Yes, you knew him. He came here to see you in connection with that lawsuit of yours."

"You're crazy!" Perry said, then catching himself, said

quickly, "I beg your pardon, Mr. Selby, I didn't mean that. You know, I was just speaking hastily. I didn't mean to be disrespectful, but the idea's all cuckoo. I never heard of the man in my life."

Sheriff Brandon said slowly, "Look here, Perry, we know that this man was interested in your lawsuit. He'd made a collection of newspaper clippings about it."

"Lots of people are interested in it," Perry said sullenly.

"But this man had some particular reason to be interested in it."

"Well, suppose he did?"

"We want to know what that interest was," Selby said.

"You'll have to ask someone else, I can't tell you."

Once more the officers exchanged glances.

"The typewriting stopped the first time you knocked on the door?"

"Yes."

"You don't know how long the typewriting had been going on?"

"No, the man was typing when I got out of the elevator."

"And you say it sounded like a machine gun?"

"I'll say it did."

"It was rapid?"

"Yes."

"Were there any pauses?"

"Not a pause. The thing was being ripped off at high speed, by someone who knew what he was doing. He could play that typewriter like my cousin could play a piano."

"And you didn't go into Helen Marks' room?"

"No, I just saw her to the door."

"How long did you stay there?"

"Just long enough to kiss her good-night."

"Did that take any great amount of time?" Brandon asked.

"What he means," Selby said, grinning, as he saw the expression on the boy's face, "is whether you had to lead up to it with any preliminaries."

"No," Perry said readily enough. "She . . . well, I think it was her idea. She sort of turned around and stuck up her chin."

"And you don't know any reason why this man was interested in your lawsuit?"

"No," Perry said, then, after a moment's hesitation, added, "I wouldn't want this repeated, but I'm afraid it isn't much of a lawsuit, Mr. Selby. I'm willing to settle for anything I can get, but I don't think I can even get an offer. I need money—need it bad."

"As I see it," Selby remarked, keeping his eyes fixed on the younger man, "the whole thing hinges on the question of whether a marriage ceremony had been performed. Now, here's a man who's a minister of the Gospel who's taken an interest in the case. Naturally, the first thought which comes to my mind is that he must have known something about a marriage ceremony."

Perry shook his head and said, "My lawyers have searched the records everywhere. It doesn't make any difference if a marriage ceremony was performed, if it wasn't a legal marriage ceremony, and the law says a marriage ceremony isn't legal unless there's been a license issued and a ceremony performed in the county where the license was issued, and then there has to be some registration made, some certificate that the marriage was performed. We've searched the records everywhere and find that the folks never even took out a license. They thought their marriage in Yuma was good."

"They might have gone out of the state somewhere and married and this man might have known about it."

"Then why didn't he get in touch with me?"

"Perhaps he intended to."

Perry shook his head and said, "No, that's out, too. The folks made one trip up to Oregon. Aside from that, they stayed right there on the home place. You know, they were pretty much stay-at-home sort of people."

"When did they go to Oregon?"

"About a year ago."

"And you're certain they didn't get married in Oregon?"

"Yes, we've traced them everywhere. Of course, Mr. Selby, I'm telling you this in strict confidence. My lawyer's putting up the best bluff he can and trying to get a settlement. He'll get half if he does, so he's working hard. I'm not supposed to tell this, but if you're interested in this preacher and figure he had anything to do with the case, I want you to have the low-down on it."

Brandon said, not unkindly, "That's all, Herbert. Go on back to the service station, and don't tell anyone you've been questioned. Just keep quiet about everything."

When Perry had closed the door behind him, the sheriff and Doug Selby hitched their chairs closer together. "The kid's telling the truth," Brandon announced.

"I know it," Selby said, "but it's such a peculiar coincidence that *he* should have been the one to knock on the door."

"Coincidences happen like that in real life all the time. Think of what a coincidence it was that the real Charles

Brower should have come walking into the hotel and found his wife there."

"That wasn't a coincidence," Selby pointed out. "There are basic reasons back of that. That's no more a coincidence than it is that a man playing a poor game of chess suddenly finds his king where he can't make a move. Brower came to the hotel to claim the money. His wife came on here to identify his remains and thought she saw a chance to collect her traveling expenses and perhaps a little extra. So she stayed on."

"Well, nothing's a coincidence if you want to look at things that way," Brandon said, "because there's a reason for everything."

Selby said slowly, "I'm wondering if there's a reason that this Marks girl picked up this particular young man and brought him to the hotel at a certain particular time."

Brandon shrugged his shoulders.

"And you can't get anything out of Brower?" Selby asked.

"Not a thing," Brandon said. "He's close-mouthed as a clam. And his wife smells a rat somewhere. She wants him to talk—but to her, and not to us. She rushed out and got him a lawyer. . . . Where do you suppose Larrabie got that five thousand dollars from?"

"That's a problem," Selby remarked. "Hang it, I never saw a case which looked so beautifully simple on the face of it. But everything we touch goes haywire. His wife says he never had five thousand dollars or five hundred dollars. If he had as much as fifty dollars ahead, he thought he was rich. They lived on starvation wages, and the church was behind in the salary much of the time. They were paid in produce, promises and abuse."

"*I* think the actress paid it," Brandon insisted.

Selby laughed. "Don't be silly. In the first place, why would she have paid it? In the second place, if she had, she isn't the kind to have lied to me about it."

"We can't be too sure," the sheriff said slowly. "People do funny things. There may have been blackmail mixed up in it."

"Not with Larrabie," Selby said. "He's too absolutely genuine. He was busy making the world a better place to live in."

"Maybe *he* was," Brandon agreed, "but I'm not so sure about Brower."

"I'm not so certain about him either," Selby admitted.

"Somehow, I think Brower's our man," Brandon said slowly. "He may have something on his mind besides the murder, but I think Brower either did it or knows who did it."

"It's funny he'd keep silent."

"He won't say a word, and his wife rushed right out and hired Roper to defend him."

"What did Roper do?"

"Demanded to see his client. Told him to keep still and not say anything, to answer no questions whatever. And then he demanded we put a charge against him or turn him loose. He claims he's going to get a writ of *habeas corpus*."

"Let him get it," Selby said, "and in the meantime we'll trace every move Brower made from the time he left Millbank until he showed up here."

The sheriff nodded. "The Los Angeles sheriff's office is going to co-operate. They never got much cooperation out of the old gang here and they're tickled to death to work with us. By tomorrow I'll know everything about Brower, whether he wants to talk or not."

He pulled the cloth tobacco sack from his pocket, opened a cigarette paper and sprinkled flakes of tobacco into the paper.

"Well," he said as he rolled the cigarette, "I wonder what *The Blade* will have to say about it tonight."

"Probably plenty," Selby admitted, then went on to say, "You can gamble on this: Brower and Larrabie hatched up some sort of scheme. Larrabie came here as a part of that scheme."

"Well, if Larrabie got the money and that was all there was to it, why didn't he go down to Los Angeles and join Brower or telephone for Brower to meet him back in Millbank? He had no business staying on here, if that's all he came for."

Selby nodded slowly.

"If you were a stranger in town, Doug, and wanted to get five thousand dollars, how would you go about it?" the sheriff asked.

Selby laughed as the sheriff, shaking the cigarette into a perfect cylinder, peered steadily at him.

"I'd hold up a bank or something."

"Or perhaps indulge in a little blackmail."

"You'd have a sweet time getting five thousand bucks in blackmail out of anyone in this town," the district attorney said. "And even then, there wouldn't be any excuse for sticking around afterwards."

"*And* in five one-thousand-dollar-bills," the sheriff remarked significantly, starting for the door. He turned as he opened the door to say, "*I* keep thinking about that actress angle. Those bills look like outside money to me."

"Forget it," Selby insisted. "I had a good heart-to-heart talk with her."

"Yeah," the sheriff remarked through a crack in the door, "you might have had a *better* perspective on the case, if you'd talked over the telephone."

He slammed the door as Selby jumped to his feet.

Selby was still scowling savagely when Amorette Standish tiptoed into the room and said, "Sylvia Martin's out there. She wants to see you."

"Show her in," Selby said, looking at his watch.

Amorette Standish held the door open and said, "Come in."

Sylvia bustled into the office with quick, business-like efficiency, a folded newspaper under her arm.

"How's it coming?" she asked. "And what's this about Brower?"

"Brower tried to claim the money at the hotel," Selby said.

"What money?"

"Five thousand dollars that was left in an envelope by Larrabie."

"You mean Larrabie had five thousand dollars?"

"Yes."

"You didn't tell me about this."

"I was keeping it a secret. I didn't know about it myself until some time after viewing the body. Cushing had the envelope in his safe. Of course, he didn't know what was in it, so he didn't consider it as being very important."

"Where did Larrabie get the five thousand dollars?"

"That," he told her, "is what we're trying to find out."

"And why did he take Brower's name?"

Selby shrugged his shoulders and said shortly, "*You* guess for a while, I'm tired."

Sylvia sat down on the edge of his desk and said, "Listen, Doug, how about that actress?"

"Oh, well," Doug said, "I may as well tell you the whole truth. I guess you were right after all. *The Blade* will publish the story, if you don't, and it's better for you to publish it the way it is than to let people read about it the way it wasn't."

He began at the beginning and told her the entire story of his meeting with Shirley Arden.

When he had finished, she said, "And there was the odor of perfume on that money?"

"Yes."

"What sort of perfume?"

"I can't tell you," he said, "but I'd know it, if I smelled it again. It was rather a peculiar perfume, a delicate blend of scents."

"That would mean the money came from a woman."

He shrugged his shoulders.

"And the only woman you know of that this man contacted was the actress."

"I don't suppose," Selby said wearily, "it would do me any good to tell you that this actress isn't the sort who would lie. She told me the truth."

"Did you," Sylvia asked, watching him with narrowed eyes, "take the precaution to find out what sort of perfume she was using?"

Selby nodded wearily and said, "I regret to say that I did."

"Why the regrets, Doug?"

"Oh, I don't know. It was cheap. It was doubting her word, somehow."

"And the perfumes weren't the same?"

There was an intent something in Sylvia's voice, like a cross-examiner getting ready to spring a trap.

Selby's voice contained a note of triumph, "I can assure you," he said, "that they were most certainly *not* the same."

Sylvia whipped from under her arm the newspaper she was carrying. She jerked it open, spread it out on the desk and said, "I don't suppose you bother to read the motion picture gossip in the Los Angeles daily periodicals."

"Good Lord, no," Selby exclaimed. "Why should I?"

Sylvia ran her finger down a syndicated column dealing with the daily doings of the motion picture stars.

"Here it is," she said. "Read it."

Selby bent forward and read:

"It's a well-known fact that people get tired of living in one house, of being surrounded by one environment. Stars feel this just the same as others. Perhaps the best illustration of that is the case of Shirley Arden's perfume.

"Miss Arden's personality has never been associated with that impulsive temperament which has characterized most stars who have won the hearts of the picture goers through the portrayal of romantic parts. Yet, upon occasion, Miss Arden can be as impulsively original in her reactions as even the most temperamental actress on the lot.

"Witness that for years Miss Arden has been exceedingly partial to a particular brand of perfume, yet, over night, she suddenly turned against that scent and gave away hundreds of dollars' worth of it to her stand-in, Lucy Molten.

"Moreover, Miss Arden would have nothing to do with garments which even bore the smell of that perfume. She sent some to be cleaned, gave others away. She ordered her perfumer to furnish her with an entirely new scent which was immediately installed on her dressing table both at home and in the studio.

"I trust that Miss Arden will forgive me for this intimate revelation which, for some reason, she apparently tried to clothe in secrecy. But it's merely one of those examples of outstanding individuality which mark the true artist."

Selby looked up into Sylvia Martin's steady eyes, then reached for the telephone.

"I want to get Shirley Arden, the picture actress, in Hollywood," he said to the operator. "If I can't get her, I'll talk with Ben Trask, her manager. Rush the call. It's important."

He slammed the telephone speaker back into its pronged rest. His lips were clamped tightly shut. His face had changed color.

Sylvia Martin looked at him for a moment, then crossed to his side and rested her hand on his shoulder.

"I'm sorry, Doug," she said, and proved the extent of her understanding and sympathy by saying nothing more.

13

Events during the next few minutes moved in a swift, kaleidoscopic fashion.

Frank Gordon entered the office, very much excited, to report a shooting scrape down on Washington Avenue.

"You'll have to go, Gordon," Selby said. "This will be a good chance for you to break in. Take a shorthand reporter with you and take down everything that's said, ask the suspect if he wants a lawyer."

Selby gave Gordon a few more instructions and sent him out. Sylvia smiled across at Selby.

"If cases would only come singly," she said, "but they don't."

"No," he told her, "they don't, and this Larrabie case is a humdinger."

The telephone rang.

"That," Selby said, squaring his jaw, "will be Ben Trask."

But it wasn't Ben Trask, it was Harry Perkins, the coroner, and for once his slow, drawling speech was keyed up to an almost hysterical pitch.

"I want you to come down here right away, Selby," he said; "there's hell to pay."

Selby stiffened in his chair.

"What's the matter?" he asked. "A murder?"

"Murder nothing. It's ten times worse than a murder," he said, "it's a dirty damn dog poisoner."

For the moment Selby couldn't believe his ears.

"Come on down to earth," he said, "and tell me the facts."

"My police dog, Rogue," the coroner said, "somebody got him, with poison. He's at the vet's now. Doc's working on him. It'll be touch and go, with one chance in ten for the dog."

He broke off with something which sounded very much as though he had choked back a sob.

"Any clews?" Selby asked.

"I don't know, I haven't had time to look. I just found him and rushed him down to the veterinary's. I'm down at Dr. Perry's hospital now."

"I'll come down and see what can be done," Selby said.

He hung up the telephone, and turned to Sylvia Martin.

"That," he said, "shows how callous we get about things which don't concern us, and how worked up we get when things get close to home. That's Harry Perkins, the coroner. He's been out on murder cases, suicides, automobile accidents and all forms of violent death. He's picked up people in all stages of delapidation, and to him it's been just one more corpse. Tears, entreaties and hysterics mean nothing to him. He's grown accustomed to them. But somebody poisoned his dog, and damned if he isn't crying."

"And you're going down to see about a poisoned dog?" Sylvia Martin asked.

"Yes."

"Good Lord, why?"

"In the first place, he feels so cut up about it, and, in a way, he's one of the official family. In the second place, he's down at Dr. Perry's Dog and Cat Hospital—you know, Dr. H. Franklin Perry, the brother who stands to inherit the money in the Perry Estate if young Herbert Perry loses out."

"Well?" she asked.

"I've never talked with Dr. Perry," Selby said. "The sheriff's office found he didn't know anything about the man who was killed and let it go at that, but somehow I want to take a look at him."

"Anything except a hunch?" she asked.

"It isn't even that," he said, "but, if that morphine was deliberately mixed in with the sleeping tablets, it must have been done by someone who had access to morphine, and who could have fixed up a tablet. Dr. Perry runs a veterinary hospital and . . ."

"Forget it," she told him. "That whole thing was a plant, along with the letter. Larrabie never took that sleeping medicine. Not voluntarily, anyway. His wife said he never had any trouble sleeping. Don't you remember?"

Selby nodded moodily.

"Moreover," she pointed out, "when it comes to suspicions, you can find lots of people to suspect."

"Meaning?" he asked.

"Meaning," she said, "that *I've* never been satisfied with this man Cushing's explanations.

"In the first place, the way he shields Shirley Arden means that in some way she's more than just a transient customer who occasionally comes up from Los Angeles. In the second place, he didn't disclose anything about that five thousand dollars in the safe until pretty late. In the third place, he was so blamed anxious to have it appear the death was accidental.

"Now, whoever wrote that letter and addressed the envelope was someone who didn't know the man's *real* identity. The only thing he knew was what he'd picked up from the hotel register.

"Therefore, the murderer must have been someone who had access to the information on the hotel register. And, aside from what he could learn from that register, he didn't know a thing about the man he killed. Therefore, he acted on the assumption that his victim was Charles Brower.

"He wanted to make the murder appear like suicide so he wrote that letter and left it in the typewriter. If the man had *really* been Charles Brower, nothing would ever have been thought of it. The post-mortem wouldn't have been continued to the extent of testing the vital organs for morphine. And, even if they had found some morphine, they'd have blamed it on the sleep medicine.

"Now the person who would have been most apt to be misled by the registration would have been the manager of the hotel."

"But what possible motive could Cushing have had for committing the murder?"

"You can't tell until you find out what the bond is between Cushing and Shirley Arden. I can't puzzle it *all* out, I'm just giving you a thought."

His eyes were moody as he said slowly, "That's the worst of messing around with one of these simple-appearing murder cases. If someone sneaked into the room and stabbed him, or had shot him, or something like that, it wouldn't have been so bad, but . . . Oh, hang it, this case *had* to come along right at the start of my term of office."

"Another thing," she said, "to remember is that the person who wrote the letter, and probably the person who committed the murder, got in there from three nineteen. Now there wasn't anyone registered in three nineteen. That means the person must have had a passkey."

"I've thought of all that," Selby said. "The murderer could hardly have come in through the transom, couldn't have come in through the door of three twenty-one, and he couldn't have come in through the door of three twenty-three—that is, what I really mean is, he couldn't have gone *out* that way. He could have gotten *in* the room by a dozen different methods. He could have been hiding in the room, he could have walked in through the door of three twenty-one, he could have gone in through three twenty-three. After all, you know, we don't know that the door wasn't barricaded *after* the man had died. From what Herbert Perry says, someone must have been in the room some two or three hours after death took place.

"But when that man went *out,* he had only *one* way to go, and that was through the door of three nineteen. If he'd gone out through three twenty-three he couldn't have bolted the door from the inside. If he'd gone out through the door of three twenty-one he couldn't have barricaded the door with a chair. There was no chance he could have gone out through the window. Therefore, three nineteen represents the only way he could have gone out."

"And he couldn't have gone out that way," she said,

"unless he'd known the room was vacant and had a passkey, and had previously left the communicating door unlocked."

"That's probably right."

"Well," she said, "it's up to you, but personally I'd be inclined to look for an inside job around the hotel somewhere, and *I* think Cushing is tied up too deeply with this motion picture actress to be above suspicion. It's a cinch she was the one furnished him the five thousand dollars."

"You might," Selby told her, "do a little work along that line, Sylvia. I wouldn't want to get hard-boiled with Cushing unless I had something to work on, because, after all, we haven't the faintest semblance of a motive. We..."

"How about robbery?"

"No, I've considered that. If it had been robbery, it would have been an easy matter for Cushing to have taken the envelope with the five thousand dollars out of the safe and substituted another one. He could have made a passable forgery of the signature. Since it wasn't Brower's signature in any event, there wouldn't have been much opportunity to detect the forgery."

She started for the door, turned to grin at him and said, "On my way. I'll let you know, if anything turns up."

"The devil of it is," he told her, "this isn't like one of those detective stories, which you can solve by merely pointing the finger of suspicion at the guilty person. This is a real life, flesh and blood murder case, where we've got to produce actual evidence which can stand up in a court of justice. I've got to find that murderer and then prove he's guilty beyond all reasonable doubt."

"And, if you don't do it?" she asked.

"Wait until you see *The Blade* tonight," he said gloomily. "I have an idea Sam Roper is going to make a statement."

She laughed and said, "Afraid you can't take it, Doug?"

"No," he told her. "That's not what's worrying me. I know damn well I can take it. What's worrying me is whether I can dish it out."

She grinned, said, "Go to it, big boy," and closed the door behind her as she left his private office.

Ten seconds later the telephone rang.

To Selby's surprise it was Shirley Arden herself at the other end of the wire.

"I think," he told her, "there are some things we need to have cleared up."

She hesitated a moment, then said, "I'd be only too glad to talk with you. It's going to be very difficult for me to come up to Madison City, and you know the position I'm in after the nasty insinuations the newspapers have made. If I showed up there now they'd have me virtually accused of murder. Couldn't *you* come down here?"

"When?"

"Tonight."

"Where?"

"You know where my house is in Beverly Hills?"

"Yes," he told her, his voice still savagely official, "I once went on a rubberneck tour. Had an old maid aunt out from the East. She wanted to see where all of the stars lived. Yours is the place that sets up on a hill, with a fountain in the front yard and the stone lions in front of the porch, isn't it?"

"That's the one. Could you be there tonight at eight?"

"Yes."

"We can have a quiet little dinner—just we two. Don't say anything about it. In other words, don't let anyone know you're coming to see me."

"Do you know what I want to see you about?" he asked.

"Haven't the least idea," she told him cheerfully, "but I'll be glad to see you under more favorable circumstances than the last visit."

"The circumstances," he announced, "won't be more favorable."

Her laugh was a throaty ripple, as she said, "My, you're so grim you frighten me. Tonight, then, at eight. Goodby." She put the receiver on the hook.

Selby grabbed for his hat and started for Dr. Perry's Dog and Cat Hospital.

Dr. Perry looked up as Selby came in. In his fifties, a man of quiet determination, he was busy at work. He had a police dog slung in canvas in a long bathtub. The dog's head had drooped forward, his tongue lolled from his mouth, and his eyes were glazed.

Dr. Perry's sleeves were rolled up, his smock was stained and splashed. In his right hand he held a long, flexible rubber tube connected with a glass tank. He slightly compressed the end of the tube and washed out the sides of the bathtub.

"That's all that can be done," he said. "I've got him thoroughly cleaned out and given him a heart stimulant. Now we'll just have to keep him quiet and see what happens."

He lifted the big dog as tenderly as though it had been a child, carried it to a warm, dry kennel on which a thick paper mattress had been spread. He made the dog as comfortable as possible, closed the kennel and said, "Now we'll go clean up the mess."

Harry Perkins blew his nose explosively. "Think he'll live?" he asked.

"I can tell you more in a couple of hours. He'd had an awful shock. You should have got him here sooner."

"I got him here just as quickly as I could. Do you know what kind of poison it was?"

"No, it was plenty powerful, whatever it was. It doesn't act like anything I've encountered before, but we've done everything possible."

"This is the district attorney," Perkins said.

Dr. Perry nodded to Selby and said, "Glad to meet you."

Perkins said, "Doug, I don't care how much it costs, I want this thing run to the ground. I want to find the man who poisoned that dog. Rogue has the nicest disposition of any dog in the world. He's friendly to everyone. Of course, he's a good watchdog. That's to be expected. If anyone tries to get in my place and touch anything, Rogue would tear him to pieces, but he knows where the property line is just as well as though he'd had it surveyed. He's particularly friendly to children. There isn't a kid in the block but what knows him and loves him."

The veterinary fitted the hose over one of the faucets in the bathtub, cleaned out the bathtub, washed off his hands and arms, took off the stained smock and said, "Well, let's go out to your place and take a look around. I want to see whether it's general poison which has been put around through the vicinity, or something which was tossed into your yard where your dog would get it."

"But why should anyone toss anything in to Rogue in particular?"

The veterinarian shrugged his shoulders. "Primarily because he's a big dog," he said. "That means when he scratches up lawns, he digs deep into the grass. It's not often people deliberately poison any particular dog unless he's a big dog, or unless it's a little dog who's vicious. Small, friendly dogs are mostly poisoned from a general campaign. Big dogs are the ones who get singled out for special attention."

"Why do people poison dogs?" Selby asked.

"For the same reason some people rob and murder," the veterinarian said. "People in the aggregate are all right, but there's a big minority that have no regard for the rights of others. In my opinion a person who would poison a dog would poison a man, if he thought he could get away with it. I'd like to see dog poisoning made a state prison offense."

"To think of a man deliberately throwing a dog poisoned food," Perkins declared, "makes my blood boil. I'd shoot a man who'd do it."

"Well, let's take a run over to your place and look around," Dr. Perry suggested. "You say the dog hasn't been out of the yard? We may find some of the poison left there and learn something from it."

"How about Rogue, can we do him any good staying here?"

"Not a bit. To tell you the truth, Harry, I think he'll pull through. I'm not making any promises, but I hope he's over the worst of it. What he needs now is rest. My assistant will keep him under close observation. Have you got your car here?"

"Yes."

"Good. We'll drive over with you."

The three of them drove to the place where Perkins had his undertaking establishment, with living quarters over the mortuary. In back of the place was a fenced yard which led to an alley. There was a gate in the alley.

"The dog stayed in here?" Dr. Perry asked.

"Yes. He's always in the building or here in the yard."

Dr. Perry walked around the backyard, looking particularly along the line of the fence. Suddenly he stooped and picked up something which appeared to be a ball of earth. He broke it open and disclosed the red of raw meat.

"There you are," he said, "a deadly little pellet. That's been mixed by a skillful dog poisoner. He put the poison in raw hamburger, then he rolled the hamburger in the earth so it would be almost impossible to see. A dog's nose would detect the raw meat through the coating of earth but your eye would be fooled by the earth which had been placed around it. Let's look around and see if we can find some more."

A survey of the yard disclosed two more of the little rolls of poisoned meat.

"Notice the way these were placed along the sides of the fence," Selby said to the coroner. "They weren't just tossed over the fence, but were deliberately placed there. That means that someone must have walked through the gate and into the back yard."

"By George, that's so," Perkins exclaimed.

"That's undoubtedly true," Dr. Perry agreed. "Now, then, if the dog were here in the yard, why didn't he bark?"

Moreover, why didn't the poisoner stand in the alley and just toss the rolls of meat in to the dog?"

Perkins turned to the district attorney and asked, "What can you do to a dog poisoner, Selby?"

"Not a great deal," Selby admitted. "It's hard to convict them, if they stand trial. And when they are convicted a judge usually gives them probation. A judge hates to send a man to jail for poisoning an animal. Usually it's a property owner and a citizen who's otherwise respected. However, being caught once usually puts a stop to the poisoning activities for some time."

"To my mind," Perry said, "they should be hung. It's a worse crime than murder."

"That's exactly the way I feel about it," Perkins agreed emphatically.

They walked back through the yard into the back room of the mortuary.

"We'd better take a look around here, too," Perry suggested. "This commences to look like an inside job to me. It looks as though someone you'd been talking to had casually strolled around here and planted this stuff. Can you remember having had anyone roaming around the place, Harry? It must have been someone who planted the poison right while you were talking with him."

"Why, yes," Perkins said, "there were several people in here. I had a coroner's jury sitting on the inquest on the man who was murdered in the hotel."

He turned to Selby and said, "That was yesterday, while you were gone. They returned a verdict of murder by person or persons unknown. I presume you knew that."

"Yes," Selby remarked. "It seems the only possible verdict which could have been returned."

He turned to Perry and said, "I'm wondering if *you* knew the dead man, Doctor."

"No, I'd never seen him in my life—not that I know of."

Selby took a photograph from his inside coat pocket, showed it to Dr. Perry.

"I wish you'd take a good look at that," he said, "and see if it looks at all familiar."

Dr. Perry studied it from several angles and slowly shook his head. "No," he said. "The sheriff asked me about him, and showed me the same picture. I told the sheriff I'd never seen him, but now, looking at this photograph, I somehow get the impression I've seen him somewhere . . . you know, the face has a vaguely familiar look. Perhaps it's just a type. I can't place him, but there's something about him that reminds me of someone."

Selby was excited. "I wish you'd think carefully," he said. "You know the man had some clippings in his brief case about the litigation you're interested in."

"Yes, the sheriff told me that he did," Perry said, "but lots of people are interested in that case. I've had lots of letters about it. You see, quite a few people got interlocutory decrees and then went into another state to get married. They're worried about where they'd stand on inheritances and such. That's probably why this man was interested . . . .But he reminds me of someone. . . . Perhaps it's a family resemblance. . . . Let me see what clippings he cut out and I may be able to tell you more about him. I must have had a hundred letters from people who sent clippings and asked for details."

"Ever answer the letters?" Selby asked.

"No. I didn't have time. It keeps me busy running my own business. Paying off the mortgage on this new hospital keeps my nose to the grindstone. I wish that lawsuit would get finished—but my lawyer says it's about over now. I couldn't pay him a regular fee, so he took it on a big contingency. He'll make almost as much out of it as I will."

"Hope he does," the coroner said. "He owes me a nice little sum on a note that's overdue."

The coroner took out the brief case, suitcase and portable typewriter. "By the way," he asked, "is it all right to deliver these to the widow? She was in to get them a while ago."

"I did that already. He says it's okay by him, if it is by you."

"Go ahead and give them to her, then. But be sure the inventory checks."

The coroner opened the suitcase, also the brief case.

"Well," Selby said, "I'm going to be getting on back to the office. Perhaps Dr. Perry can tell us something after his examination of those poisoned scraps."

"Wait a minute," the veterinarian said, laying down the newspaper clippings the coroner had handed him, "what's that over there in the corner?"

Perkins stared, then said, "Good Lord, it's another one of the same things."

They walked over and picked it up. Perry examined it then dropped it into his pocket.

"That settles it," he announced. "It was aimed directly at your dog and it's an inside job, someone who's been in here today. Can you remember who was in here?"

"The last man in here today," Perkins said, "was George

Cushing, manager of the Madison Hotel. It's a cinch *he* wouldn't have done anything like that."

"No," Selby said, "we'd hardly put Cushing in the category of a dog poisoner."

"Who else?" the veterinarian asked.

"Mrs. Larrabie was in here, the dead man's widow. She looked over the things in the suitcase and in the brief case.... And Fred Lattaur, your lawyer. He came in to tell me he'd pay off my note when he had your case settled. He wouldn't have any reason to poison the dog."

"Let's take a look around and see if we can find some more," Dr. Perry said. "We can speculate afterward. Each one of us take a room. Make a thorough search."

They looked through the rooms and Selby found another of the peculiarly distinctive bits of poisoned meat.

"Anyone else been in here today?" Selby demanded. "Think carefully, Perkins. It's important. There's more to this than appears on the surface."

"No.... Wait a minute, Mrs. Brower was in. *She's* on the war path," the coroner said. "She thought I had five thousand dollars that had been taken from the hotel. She insists that it's her husband's money."

"Did she say where he got it?"

"She said Larrabie had Brower's wallet, and that the five thousand-dollar bills had been in Brower's wallet. Therefore, Brower was entitled to them."

"What did she want you to do?" Selby asked.

"She wanted me to give her the money. When I told her I didn't have it, she wanted to take a look at the wallet. She said she could tell whether it was her husband's."

"Did you show it to her?"

"The sheriff has it. I sent her up to the sheriff's office."

Selby said abruptly, "You can give the rest of the stuff back to Mrs. Larrabie, Harry. I'm going to take that camera. Tell her she can have the camera in a day or two, but I want to see if there are any exposed films in it. They might furnish a clew. I've been too busy to give them any thought, but they *may* be important."

"A darned good idea," the coroner said. "That chap came down here from the northern part of the state. He probably took photographs en route. Those camera fiends are just the kind to put their friends on the front steps of the capitol building at Sacramento and take a bunch of snapshots. You may find something there that'll be worth while."

Selby nodded and pocketed the camera.

"You let me know about that dog," Perkins said anxiously to the veterinarian. Then he turned to Selby. "I want something done about this poisoning. At least drag these people who've been in here in for questioning. And *I'd* start with Mrs. Brower. She looks mean to me."

"I'll give you a ring in an hour or two," Selby promised. "I'm pretty busy on that murder case, but I have a hunch this poisoning business may be connected somehow with that case. I'll do everything I can."

"It's commencing to look," Dr. Perry said, "as though this wasn't any casual poisoning, but something that had been carefully planned to get Rogue out of the way. I'd guard this place day and night for a while, if I were you, Perkins."

Selby said, "Good idea," and left Perkins and the veterinarian talking as he started for his office.

14

Selby felt absurdly conspicuous as he parked his car in front of the actress's residence. There was something about the quiet luxury of the place which made the stone Peiping lions on either side of the porch stairway seem as forbidding as vicious watchdogs, frozen into immobility by the temporary command of a master, but ready at any moment to rush forth and repel an intruder.

Selby climbed the stairs. The vine-covered porch gave a hint of cool privacy for the hot days of summer.

A military butler, with broad, straight shoulders, thin waist and narrow hips, opened the door almost as soon as Selby's finger touched the bell button. Looking past him to the ornate magnificence of the reception hallway and the living room which opened beyond, Selby felt once more that touch of awkward embarrassment, a vague feeling of being out of place.

That feeling was dissipated by the sight of Shirley Arden.

She was wearing a cocktail gown, and he noticed with satisfaction, that, while there was a touch of formality in her attire, it was only the semi-formality with which one would receive an intimate friend. When she came toward him she neither presumed too much on their previous acquaintance, nor was she distant. She gave him her hand and said, "So glad you could come, Mr. Selby. We'd probably have felt a little more businesslike if we'd dined in one of the cafés, but under the circumstances, it wouldn't do for us to be seen together.

"The spaciousness of all of this is more or less a setting. I have to do quite a bit of entertaining, you know. The two of us would rattle around in here like two dry peas in a paper bag, so I've told Jarvis to set a table in the den."

She slipped her arm through his and said, "Come on and look around. I'm really proud of the architecture."

She showed him through the house, switching lights on as she walked. Selby had a confused, blurred recollection of spacious rooms, of a patio with a fountain, a private swimming pool with lights embedded in the bottom of the tank so that a tinted glow suffused the water, basement sport rooms with pool, billiard and ping-pong tables, a cocktail room with a built-in bar, mirrors and oil paintings which were a burlesque on the barroom paintings of the Nineties.

They finished their tour in a comfortable little book-lined den, with huge French doors opening out to a corner of a patio on one side, the other three sides lined with bookcases, the books leather-backed, de luxe editions. There were deep lounging chairs, a davenport, coffee tables, and, in the center of the room, a table had been set for two, with rose-shaded lights shedding a diffused radiance over the white cloth and the glitter of silver.

Shirley Arden motioned him to a seat, flung herself into one of the chairs, raised her feet to an ottoman with a carelessly intimate display of legs.

She stretched out her arms and said wearily, "Lord, but it was a trying day at the studio. How's the district attorney business going?"

"Not so good," he told her, his voice uncompromisingly determined.

The butler brought them cocktails and a tray of appetizers, which he set on the coffee table between them. As they clicked the rims of their glasses, Selby noticed the butler placing the huge silver cocktail shaker, beaded with frosty moisture, upon the table.

"I don't go in for much of this, you know. And, after all, this visit is official," Selby said.

"Neither do I," she told him, laughing, "but don't get frightened at the size of the container. That's just Hollywood hospitality. Don't drink any more than you want. There's an inner container in that cocktail shaker, so the drink will keep cold as ice without being diluted by melting ice. You can have just as much or as little as you want.

"You know, we who are actively working in pictures don't dare to do much drinking. It's the people who are slipping on the downward path toward oblivion who hit it heavy. And there are always a lot of hangers-on who can punish the liquor. Try some of those anchovy tarts with the cream cheese around them. They're really good— Jarvis's specialty."

Selby began to feel more at home. The cocktail warmed him, and there was a delightful informality about Shirley Arden which made the spacious luxury of the house seem something reserved for more formal occasions, while the warm intimacy of this little den gave the impression of having been created entirely for Selby's visit. He found it impossible to believe her capable of deceit.

She put down her empty cocktail glass, smiled and said unexpectedly, with the swift directness of a meteor shooting across the night sky, "So you wanted to see me about the perfume?"

"How did you know?" he asked.

"I knew perfume entered into the case somewhere," she said, "because of the very apparent interest you took in the perfume I used.

"As a matter of fact, I changed my perfume either one or two days before, I've forgotten which, on the advice of an astrologer. You don't believe in astrology, do you?"

He didn't answer her question directly, but asked, "*Why* did you change your perfume?"

"Because I was informed that the stars threatened disaster, if I didn't. . . . Oh, I know it sounds so stupid when one says it that way, but there are lots of things which seem perfectly logical in the privacy of your own mind which look like the devil when you bring them out into public conversation. Don't you think so?"

"Go on," he told her, "I'm listening."

She laughed and flexed her muscles as some cat might twist and stretch in warm sunlight, not the stretch of weariness, but that sinuous, twisting stretch of excess animal vitality seeking outlet through muscular activity.

"Do you know," she said, "we are hopelessly ignorant about the most simple things of life. Take scent, for instance. A flower gives forth a scent. A man gives forth a scent. Every living thing has some odor associated with it. I can walk down this path," and she made a sweeping, graceful gesture toward the patio beyond the French windows, "with my feet encased in leather. Each foot rests on the ground for only a fifth of a second, if I'm walking rapidly. Yet my life force throws off vibrations. The very ground I have walked on starts vibrating in harmony with the rhythm of my own vibrations. We can prove that by having a bloodhound start on my trail. His nose is attuned to the vibrations which we call odor, or scent. He can detect unerringly every place where I have put my foot.

"Women use scent to enhance their charm. It emphasizes in some way the vibrations they are casting forth, vibrations which are emanating all of the time. One scent will go fine with one personality, yet clash with another. Do you see what I mean?"

"I'm still listening," Selby told her. " . . . And the anchovy tarts *are* delicious."

She laughed, glanced swiftly at him. There was almost a trace of fear in her eyes and more than a trace of nervousness in her laugh.

"There's something about you," she said, "which frightens me. You're so . . . so damned, persistently direct."

"Rude?" he asked.

"No," she said, "it's not rudeness. It's a positive, vital something. You're boring directly toward some definite objective in everything you do."

"We were talking," he told her, "about the reason you changed your perfume."

"For some time," she said, "I've known that I was— well, let us say, out of step with myself. Things haven't been going just right. There were numerous little irritations which ordinarily I'd have paid no attention to. But recently they began to pile up. I began to lose that inner harmony, that sense of being in tune with the rhythm of existence . . . if you know what I mean?"

"I think I understand, yes."

"I went to an astrologer. She told me that my personality was undergoing a change, and I can realize she's correct. Now that I look back on it, I think every successful picture actress goes through at least two distinct phases of development. Very few of us are born to the purple. We're usually recruited from all walks of life, stenographers, waitresses, artists' models. We're a peculiar lot. We nearly always have a wild streak, which makes us break loose into an unconventional form of life. I don't mean immorality, I mean lack of conventional routine.

"Then we get a try-out. We're given minor parts. We are given a major part. If it's a poor story, with poor direction and poor support, that's all there is to it. But occasionally it's a good story, with good direction, something outstanding. A new personality is flashed on the screen to the eyes of theater-goers, and the effect is instantaneous. Millions of people all over the world suddenly shower approval upon that new star."

He nodded.

"Let me fill up your cocktail glass."

"No," he told her, "one's plenty."

"Oh, come on," she coaxed, "have half a one. I want one more and I don't want to feel conspicuous."

"Just half a one, then," he said.

She didn't try to take advantage of his acquiescence, but was scrupulously careful to pause when his glass was half full. She filled her own, raised it to her lips and sipped it appreciatively.

"I'm trying to tell you this in detail," she said, "because I'm so darned anxious to have you understand me and to understand my problems."

"And the reason for changing the perfume," he reminded her.

"Don't worry," she remarked, "I won't try to dodge the question—not with such a persistent cross-examiner."

"Well, anyway, an actress finds herself catapulted into fame, almost overnight. The public takes a terrific interest in her. If she goes out to a restaurant, she's pointed out and stared at. On the street, people driving automobiles suddenly recognize her and crane their necks in complete disregard of traffic. The fan magazines are crazy to satisfy reader demand for a new star. They'll write up anything they can find.

"Of course, lots of it's hooey. Lots of it isn't. People are interested. I'm not conceited enough to think they're interested entirely in the star. They're interested in the spectacle of some fellow mortal being shot up into wealth, fame and success—the eternal Cinderella story.

"No wonder a star's personality changes. She emerges from complete obscurity, drab background and usually a very meager idea of the formalities, into the white light of publicity. Visiting notables want to lunch with her; money pours in on her; there's pomp, glitter, the necessity of a complete readjustment. An actress either breaks under that, or she achieves poise. When she achieves poise, she's become a different personality in a way."

"And why did you change your perfume?"

"Because I've passed through that stage and didn't realize it. I'd been using the same perfume for months. And during those months I've been undergoing a transition of personality."

She pressed an electric button. Almost instantly the butler appeared with a steaming tureen of soup.

"Let's eat," she said, smiling. "We're having just a little informal dinner. No elaborate banquet."

He seated her at the table. The butler served the soup. When he had retired, she smiled across at Selby and said, "Now that that's explained, what else do we talk about?"

Selby said slowly, "We talk about the brand of perfume you used before you made the change, and whether you were still using this same brand of perfume on last Monday, when you stayed at the Madison Hotel. And we once more talk about *why* you made the change."

She slowly lowered her spoon to her plate. The elation had vanished from her manner.

"Go ahead and eat," she said wearily, "we'll talk it over after dinner—if we must."

"You should have known," he told her, "that we must."

She sighed, picked up her spoon, tried to eat the soup, but her appetite had vanished. When the butler removed her soup dish it was more than two-thirds filled.

A steak, vegetables, salad and dessert were perfectly cooked and served. Selby was hungry, and ate. Shirley

ERLE STANLEY GARDNER

Arden was like some woman about to be led to the executioner and enduring the irony of that barbaric custom which decrees that one about to die shall be given an elaborate repast.

She tried to keep up conversation, but there was no spontaneity to her words. The radiant personality which emanated from her so powerfully it could be caught by the camera and transferred to the screen had vanished.

At length, when the dessert had been finished and the butler served a liqueur, she raised her eyes to Selby and said with lips which seemed to be on the verge of trembling, "Go ahead."

"What perfume did you use on Monday, the old or the new?"

"The old," she said.

"Precisely what," he asked her, shooting one question at her when she expected another, "is your hold on George Cushing?"

She remained smiling, but her nostrils slightly dilated. She was breathing heavily. "I didn't know that I had any hold on him," she said.

"Yes, you did," Selby told her. "You have a hold on him and you use it. You go to Madison City and he protects your incognito."

"Wouldn't any wise hotel manager do that same thing?"

"I know Cushing," Selby said. "I know there's some reason for what he does."

"All right," she said wearily, "I have a hold on him. And the perfume which you smelled on the five thousand dollars was the perfume which I used. And Cushing telephoned to me in Los Angeles to warn me that you were suspicious; that you'd found out I'd been at the hotel; that you thought the five thousand-dollar bills had been given to Larrabie by me. So what?"

For a moment Selby thought she was going to faint. She swayed in her chair. Her head drooped forward.

"Shirley!" he exclaimed, unconscious that he was using her first name.

His hand had just touched her shoulder when a pane of glass in the French window shattered. A voice called, "Selby! Look here!"

He looked up to see a vague shadowy figure standing outside the door. He caught a glimpse of something which glittered, and then a blinding flash dazzled his eyes. Involuntarily, he blinked and, when he opened his eyes, it seemed that the illumination in the room was merely a half darkness. The twin spots of rose-colored light marking the rose-shaded table lamps was the only illumination which could register on the seared retina of his eyes.

He closed his eyes, rubbed them. Gradually, the details of the room swam back into his field of vision. He saw Shirley Arden, her arms on the table, her head drooped forward on her arm. He saw the shattered glass of the windowpane, the dark outline of the French doors.

Selby ran to the French door, jerked it open. His eyes, rapidly regaining their ability to see, strained themselves into the half darkness.

He saw the outlines of the huge house, stretching in the form of an open "U" around the patio, the swimming pool with its colored lights, the fountain which splashed water down into a basin filled with water lilies, porch swings, tables shaded by umbrellas, reclining chairs—but he saw no sign of motion.

From the street, Selby heard the quick rasp of a starting motor, the roar of an automobile engine, and then the snarling sound of tires as the car shot away into the night.

Selby turned back toward the room. Shirley Arden was as he had left her. He went toward her, placed a hand on her shoulder. Her flesh quivered beneath his hand.

"I'm sorry," he said, "it's just one of those things. But you'll have to go through with it now."

He heard the pound of heavy, masculine steps, heard the excited voice of the butler, then the door of the den burst open and Ben Trask, his face twisted with emotion, stood glaring on the threshold.

"You cheap shyster!" he said. "You damned publicity-courting, double-crossing . . ."

Selby straightened, came toward him.

"Who the devil are you talking to?" he asked.

"You!"

Shirley Arden was on her feet with a quick, panther-like motion. She dashed between the two men, pushed against Trask's chest with her hands. "No, no, Ben!" she exclaimed. "Stop it! You don't understand. Can't you see . . . ?"

"The devil I don't understand," he said. "I understand everything."

"I told him," she said. "I *had* to tell him."

"Told him what?"

"Told him about Cushing, about . . ."

"Shut up, you little fool."

Selby, stepping ominously forward, said, "Just a minute,

Trask. While you may not realize it, this visit is in my official capacity and ..."

"You and your official capacity both be damned!" Trask told him. "You deliberately engineered a cheap publicity stunt. You wanted to drag Shirley Arden into that hick town murder inquiry of yours so you'd get plenty of publicity. You deliberately imposed on her to set the stage, and then you arranged to have one of your local news-hounds come on down to take a flashlight.

"Can't you see it, Shirley?" Trask pleaded. "He's double-crossed you. He's ..."

Selby heard his voice saying with cold fury, "You, Trask, are a damned liar."

Trask pushed Shirley Arden away from him with no more effort than if she had been some gossamer figure without weight or substance.

He was a big, powerful man, yet he moved with the swiftness of a heavyweight pugilist and, despite his rage, his advance was technically correct—left foot forward, right foot behind, fists doubled, right arm across his stomach, left elbow close to the body.

Something in the very nature of the man's posture warned Selby what to expect. He was dealing with a trained fighter.

Trask's fist lashed out in a swift, piston-like blow for Selby's jaw.

Selby remembered the days when he had won the conference boxing championship for his college. Automatically his rage chilled until it became a cold, deadly, driving purpose. He moved with swift machine-like efficiency, pivoting his body away from the blow, and, at the same time, pushing out with his left hand just enough to catch Trask's arm, throw Trask off balance and send the fist sliding over his shoulder.

Trask's face twisted with surprise. He swung his right up in a vicious uppercut, but Selby, with the added advantage of being perfectly balanced, his weight shifted so that his powerful body muscles could be brought into play, smashed over a terrific right.

His primitive instincts were to slam his fist for Trask's face, just as a person yielding to a blind rage wants to throw caution to the winds, neglect to guard, concentrate only on battering the face of his opponent. But Selby's boxing training was controlling his mind. His right shot out straight for Trask's solar-plexus.

He felt his fist strike the soft, yielding torso, saw Trask bend forward and groan.

From the corner of his eye, Selby was conscious of Shirley Arden, her rigid forefinger pressed against the electric pushbutton which would summon the butler.

Trask staggered to one side, lashed out with a right which grazed the point of Selby's jaw, throwing him momentarily off balance.

He heard Shirley Arden's voice screaming, "Stop it, stop it! Both of you! Stop it! Do you hear?"

Selby sidestepped another blow, saw that Trask's face was gray with pain, saw a rush of motion as the broad-shouldered butler came running into the room, saw Shirley Arden's outstretched forefinger pointing at Trask. "Take *him,* Jarvis," she said.

The big butler hardly changed his stride. He went forward into a football tackle.

Trask, swinging a terrific left, was caught around the

waist and went down like a tenpin. A chair crashed into splintered kindling beneath the impact of the two men.

Selby was conscious of Shirley Arden's blazing eyes.

"Go!" she commanded.

The butler scrambled to his feet. Trask dropped to the floor, his hands pressed against his stomach, his face utterly void of color.

"Just a minute," Selby said to the actress, conscious that he was breathing heavily. "You have some questions to answer."

"Never!" she blazed.

Trask's voice, sounding flat and toneless, said, "Don't be a damned fool, Shirley. He's framed it all. Can't you see?"

The butler turned hopefully toward Selby.

"Don't try it, my man," Selby said.

He appreciated, however, what a formidable antagonist the man would be, realized suddenly that those broad shoulders, the thin waist and lean, muscular hips meant something. The man was evidently a bodyguard in the pink of condition.

It was Shirley Arden who pushed Jarvis back.

"No," she said, "there's no necessity for any more violence. Mr. Selby is going to leave."

She came toward him, stared up at him.

"To think," she said scornfully, "that *you'd* resort to a trick like this. Ben warned me not to trust you. He said you'd deliberately planned to let the news leak out to the papers; that you were trying to put pressure on me until I'd break. I wouldn't believe him. And now . . . this . . . this despicable trick.

"I respected you. Yes, if you want to know it, I admired you. Admired you so damned much I couldn't be normal when I was with you. Ben told me I was losing my head like a little school girl.

"You were so poised, so certain of yourself, so absolutely straightforward and wholeheartedly sincere that you seemed like pure gold against the fourteen-carat brass I'd been associating with in Hollywood. And now you turn out to be just as rotten and just as lousy as the rest of them. Get out!"

"Now, listen," Selby said, "I'm . . ."

The butler stepped forward. "You heard what she told you," he said ominously. "Get out!"

Shirley Arden turned on her heel.

"He'll get out, Jarvis," she said wearily. "You won't have to put him out—but see that he leaves."

"Miss Arden, please," Selby said, stepping forward, "you can't . . ."

The big butler tensed his muscles. "Going someplace," he said ominously, "besides out?"

Shirley Arden, without once looking back over her shoulder, left the room. Ben Trask scrambled to his feet.

"Watch him, Jarvis," Trask warned, "He's dynamite. What the hell did you tackle *me* for?"

"She said to," the butler remarked, coolly, never taking his eyes off Selby.

"She's gone nuts over him," Trask said.

"Get out," the butler remarked to Selby.

Selby knew when he was faced with hopeless odds.

"Miss Arden," he said, "is going to be questioned. If

she gives me an audience now, that questioning will take place here. If she doesn't, it will take place before the grand jury in Madison City. You *gentlemen* pay your money and take your choice."

"It's already paid," the butler said. "Get out!"

Selby started toward the front of the house. Trask came limping behind him.

"Don't think *you're* so much," Trask said sneeringly. "You may be a big toad in a small puddle, but you've got a fight on your hands now. You'll get no more co-operation out of us. And remember another thing. There's a hell of a lot of money invested in Shirley Arden. That money buys advertising in the big metropolitan newspapers. They're going to print *our* side of this thing, not yours."

The butler said evenly, "Shut up, Trask, you're making a damned fool of yourself."

He handed Selby his hat and gloves; his manner became haughtily deferential as he said, "Shall I help you on with your coat, sir?"

"Yes," Selby told him.

Selby permitted the man to adjust the coat about his neck. He leisurely drew on his gloves, nodded and said, "The door, Jarvis."

"Oh, certainly," the butler remarked sarcastically, holding open the door, bowing slightly from the waist.

Selby marched across the spacious porch, down the front steps which led to the sloping walk.

"And don't think you can get away with . . ." Ben Trask's voice was interrupted by the slamming of the door.

15

Selby found that he couldn't get the developed negatives from the miniature camera until the next morning at nine o'clock. He went to a hotel, telephoned Rex Brandon and said, "I've uncovered a lead down here, Rex, which puts an entirely new angle on the case. George Cushing is mixed in it some way, I don't know just how much.

"Cushing knew that the five thousand dollars came from Shirley Arden. He's the one who warned her to change her perfume after he knew I was going to try and identify the bills from the scent which was on them."

"You mean the money actually *did* come from the actress?" Rex Brandon asked.

"Yes," Selby said wearily.

"I thought you were certain it didn't."

"Well, it did."

"You mean she lied to you?"

"That's what it amounts to."

"You aren't going to take that sitting down, are you?"

190

"I am not."

"What else did she say?"

"Nothing."

"Well, *make* her say something."

"Unfortunately," Selby said, "that's something which is easier said than done. As was pointed out to me in a conversation a short time ago, we're fighting some very powerful interests.

"In the first place, Shirley Arden's name means a lot to the motion picture industry, and the motion picture industry is financed by banks controlled by men who have a lot of political influence.

"I'm absolutely without authority down here. The only way we can get Shirley Arden where she has to answer questions is to have her subpoenaed before the grand jury."

"You're going to do that?"

"Yes. Get a subpoena issued and get it served."

"Will she try to avoid service?"

"Sure. Moreover, they'll throw every legal obstacle in our way that they can. Get Bob Kentley, my deputy, to be sure that subpoena is legally air-tight."

"How about the publicity angle?"

"I'm afraid," Selby said, "the publicity angle is something that's entirely beyond our control. The fat's in the fire now. The worst of it is they think that I was responsible for it. Miss Arden thinks I was trying to get some advertisement."

"What do you mean?"

"Someone—I suppose it was Bittner—took a flashlight

photograph of me dining tête-à-tête with Shirley Arden in her home."

"That sort of puts you on a spot," the sheriff sympathized.

"Are you telling me?" Selby asked bitterly. "Anyway, it's absolutely ruined any possibility of co-operation at this end."

"How about Cushing? What'll we do with him?"

"Put the screws down on him."

"He'll resent it, you know."

"He isn't going to resent what we'll do to him half as much as I resent what he's done to us."

"He's been one of our staunchest supporters."

"I don't give a damn what he's been. Get hold of him and give him the works. I'm going to get those pictures in the camera developed and then I'll be up in the morning. In the meantime I'm going out to a show and forget that murder case."

"Better try a burlesque, son," the sheriff advised. "You sound sort of disillusioned. You weren't falling for that actress, were you?"

"Go to the devil," Selby said. " . . . Say, Rex . . ."

"What?"

"Give Sylvia Martin the breaks on that Cushing end of the story. She's the one who originally smelled a rat there."

"What do you mean?"

"Talk with her. Get her ideas. They may not be so bad. I thought they were haywire when she first spilled them. Now I think she's on the right track."

Selby hung up the phone, took a hot bath, changed his

clothes and felt better. He went to the movies, but scarcely followed the picture. There was a chilled, numb feeling in the back of his mind, the feeling of one who has had ideals shattered, who has lost confidence in a friend, and a sense of vague, impending disaster hung over him.

After the show, he aimlessly tramped the streets for more than an hour, paused to have a drink at a bar which was filled with gaily chatting, laughing people. Then he returned to his room.

As he opened the door and groped for the light switch, he was filled with a vague sense of uneasiness. For a moment he couldn't determine the source of that feeling of danger. Then he realized that the odor of cigar smoke was clinging to the room.

Selby didn't smoke cigars. Someone who did smoke cigars was either in the room or had been in it.

Selby found the light switch, pressed it and braced himself against the rush of an attack.

There was no one in the room.

Selby entered the room, kicked the door shut behind him and made certain that it was bolted. He was on the point of barricading it with a chair, when he remembered the room in which William Larrabie had met his death.

Feeling absurdly self-conscious, the district attorney got to his knees and peered under the bed. He saw nothing. He tried the doors to the connecting rooms and made certain they were both bolted on the inside. He opened the window and looked out. The fire escape was not near enough to furnish a means of ingress.

His baggage consisted of a single light handbag. It was

on the floor where he had left it, but Selby noticed on the bedspread an oblong imprint with the dots of four round depressions in the corners.

He picked up his handbag, looked at the bottom. There were round brass studs in each corner. Carefully, he fitted the bag to the impression on the bedspread. Beyond any doubt, someone had placed the bag on the bed. Selby knew that he had not done so.

He opened the bag. It showed that it had been searched, and searched hurriedly. Apparently the contents had been dumped onto the bed, then thrown back helter-skelter.

Selby stood staring at it in puzzled scrutiny.

Why should anyone have searched his handbag?

What object of value did he have? The search had been hasty and hurried, showing that the man who made it had been fighting against time, apparently afraid that Selby would return to the room in time to catch the caller at his task. But, not having found what he looked for, the man had overcome his fear of detection sufficiently to remain and make a thorough search of the room. That much was evident by the reek of cigar smoke which saturated the atmosphere.

The prowler had probably lit a cigar to steady his nerves. Then he had evidently made a thorough search, apparently looking for some object which had been concealed. Selby pulled back the bedspread.

The pillows had lost that appearance of starched symmetry which is the result of a chambermaid's deft touch. Evidently they had been moved and replaced.

Suddenly the thought of the miniature camera crashed home to Selby's consciousness.

He had left the camera at the camera store where the man had promised, in view of Selby's explanation of his position and the possible significance of the films, to have the negatives ready by morning. Evidently that camera was, then, of far greater importance than he had originally assumed.

Selby opened the windows and transom in order to air out the cigar smoke. He undressed, got into bed and was unable to sleep. Finally, notwithstanding the fact that he felt utterly ludicrous in doing so, he arose, walked in bare feet across the carpet, picked up a straightbacked chair, dragged it to the door and tilted it in such a way that the back was caught under the doorknob—in exactly the same manner in which the dead minister had barricaded his room on the night of the murder.

16

Selby awakened to find sun streaming into his room. He looked at the chair propped against the knob of the door and laughed outright at his fears of the night before.

A cold shower made him feel much better. He shaved, breakfasted at a restaurant, and was at the camera store by the time it opened. It was with a feeling of relief that he saw the clerk produce a roll of films from a drawer and slip them into an envelope.

"There was also a camera," Selby said.

"We have it here," the clerk nodded, and handed over the camera with its leather case.

Selby pocketed the camera. "I wonder," he asked, "if there's some place where I could look at these films?"

"Certainly," the clerk said, and switched on a light back of a ground glass.

Selby spread out the roll.

"Only fifteen of the negatives were exposed," the clerk said.

Selby nodded, and stared in puzzled bewilderment at the negatives. Without exception, they were pictures of street scenes, and, as Selby studied them, he realized that the street scenes had all been taken in Madison City.

So this, then, was merely another blank wall.

"Would you wish a magnifying glass?" the clerk asked. He handed Selby a powerful magnifier on a stand which fitted over the strip of film.

Selby bent to the films and slid them through the magnifier one at a time. He recognized familiar street scenes.

Suddenly he paused to stare at the end picture on the roll.

"Look here," he said to the clerk, "was this the *first* picture?"

The clerk looked at it and nodded.

"And it was impossible for these others to have been exposed *before* this picture was taken?"

That's right."

The picture showed a street scene, showed street car tracks, the Madison Hotel; showed, moreover, an ornamental lamp post in position at the corner.

That lamp post was being erected when Selby had gone to the hotel to inspect the body of the dead minister!

In other words, every picture in that camera had been taken long after the owner of the camera had died!

The clerk, seeing the expression on his face, said, "Was there something?"

Selby shook his head, slowly rolled up the films and put them in the metal container the clerk handed him.

"Rather nice exposures," the clerk said. "Perfectly timed."

Selby nodded, and sought the street.

Once more, what apparently had been a simple case had taken a baffling turn and he was faced with a complete impossibility, dressed, however, in the garb of such everyday plausibility that it seemed as though his own senses must be at fault.

17

Having returned to Madison City, Selby left his car in the garage to be serviced and walked up to the courthouse. On the way he had an opportunity to realize how fickle is public opinion.

While Madison City had been divided into two hostile camps over the election of district attorney and sheriff, Selby had commanded the respect of his enemies as well as the admiration and loyal support of his friends. Now he found himself in an entirely different status.

The Blade had put out an extra. Selby had stopped at a newsstand near the city limits to pick one up. It had been worse than he had anticipated.

The photograph was damning. There was the table arranged for a tête-à-tête. The actress was slumped forward in an attitude of dejection. Selby's outstretched arm seemed on the point of encircling her shoulders in a caressing gesture.

Worse than all, he had been made to appear ludicrous.

When the photographer had called his name and he had looked up to experience the blinding glare of the flashlight, he had been both startled and surprised.

Photographs of human beings under the stress of emotion almost invariably show strained, distorted expressions which appear as a gross caricature of the individual. The face of a runner breasting the tape in a hundred-yard dash, the face of a man behind the steering wheel of an automobile, making a frenzied attempt to avoid a collision, all show features which are recognizable, yet which are so twisted and distorted as to appear ludicrous.

Selby's face in the photograph showed surprise, consternation and dismay.

The garage attendant, usually so genial, so proud of having supported Selby in the election, was very much engrossed in inspecting a cut in an automobile tire. Men who ordinarily would have insisted upon Selby stopping to chat for a moment, or would have made some comment on the recent election, hurried by with scant nods, each engrossed with some suddenly urgent business which prevented him from being seen talking to the district attorney.

Selby, his jaw set grimly, strode down the flagged corridor of the big courthouse, pushed open the door of his offices and nodded to Amorette Standish.

"Sheriff Brandon called," she told him, "and wanted me to be sure to tell you, as soon as you came in, that Mr. Cushing had hurriedly left town on business."

Selby frowned, said, "Thanks," and opened the door to his private office.

Sylvia Martin was seated in his swivel chair, her feet up on his desk, her skirts showing a generous expanse of very shapely calf. She was blowing smoke rings at the ceiling.

At the sound of the opening door, she jerked her feet down and jumped from the chair with guilty consternation on her features.

"How did *you* get in here?" Selby asked, and his mood was sufficiently savage so that his voice lashed out at her bitterly.

She laughed, and said, "I sneaked in. I wanted to be the first to see you."

"Wanted to say, 'I told you so,' I suppose?" he asked.

Her eyes showed her hurt. "Doug!" she said simply.

"Well, go ahead," he told her, "get it over with. Go on, tell me I let myself get bamboozled by an actress. Tell me you warned me, but I wouldn't listen. Tell me . . ."

She came toward him, placed the tips of soft fingers against his lips. "Doug," she said, "please."

He saw then that her eyes were filling with tears.

"Don't be silly," she said, "and . . . and don't doubt me."

"I'm sorry, Sylvia," he said. "I guess I've got my fighting clothes on and I'm just looking around for heads to crack."

The dejection faded from her face. Her eyes brightened, smiled through the tears.

"Oh, swell!" she said.

"Meaning?" he asked.

"Meaning," she said, "that that was just what I was hoping you'd do. That's the only way to take it. Take it right on the chin and take it fighting."

"At that," he said, "I was an awful sap."

"No, you weren't," she protested.

"Well," he told her, "I'm in a mess now, anyway."

She nodded and said, "Let's not kid ourselves. You're in an *awful* mess, Doug. *The Blade* is clamoring for your recall, claiming that you're absolutely incompetent to solve even an ordinary mystery."

"Ordinary mystery!" he exclaimed. "This is the damnedest nightmare I ever heard of. Everything you touch flies up and hits you in the face. Even the most simple things have a way of turning themselves wrongside out, and becoming something entirely different."

"Nevertheless," she told him, looking at her watch, "you have until four-fifteen to solve it."

"Four-fifteen!" he echoed. "Why the four-fifteen?"

"Because that's the deadline of our extra."

"You're putting out an extra?"

"Yes," she said. "Want to see the headlines? I got the boss to set them up and I pulled a proof."

She opened her purse, pulled out a strip of newspaper flimsy, and stretched it across the desk. In huge black letters appeared the headline, "SELBY SOLVES MURDER."

"What's the idea?" he asked.

"The idea is," she told him, "that if *The Blade* comes out with its regular issue tonight, following up the extra this morning, you'll be finished. Public sentiment has swung definitely against you, Doug. If you once let it crystallize, it's going to be almost impossible to change it. But we'll have an extra on the street which will just about coincide with the evening edition of *The Blade*. *The Blade* will be damning you up one side and down the other. We'll have the real solution of the murder printed. It'll give the whole city a great laugh."

"I'll say it would. It would give *me* a great laugh."

"Why?"

"Because," he told her, "it's absolutely impossible to solve it. Cushing is mixed up in it and Cushing's skipped out. The actress is mixed up in it, God knows how deeply, and she won't talk. She'll avoid service of a subpoena. Probably she's taking a plane right now, flying to some seaport where she can take a trip for her health.

"Charles Brower probably knows something about her, but Sam Roper's had him released on *habeas corpus*. We didn't have enough to put a charge against him. He merely claimed the five thousand dollars belonged to him. For all we know, it does. In trying to secure possession of it, he *may* have been seeking to secure possession of his own property. He merely refuses to state where the money came from or how it happened to be in the possession of the dead man. He claims it's a business matter which doesn't concern us. That's no crime. And as long as Sam Roper is his lawyer, he won't talk. Eventually, we'll get the low-down on him, but it'll take lots of time. Even then, it'll be guesswork. What we need is proof.

"If I try to link Shirley Arden with that murder, either directly or indirectly, I'll be fighting the interests of some of the biggest bankers and financiers in the country. I'll be bucking politicians who have not only a state but a national influence. And I'll be advertising myself as a sucker. The thing's got to be fought out by a slow, dogged, persistent campaign."

She was standing close to him. Suddenly she reached up and shook him.

"Oh, you make me so damned mad!" she exclaimed.

"What's the matter?" he asked.

"Looking at it that way," she told him, "by the time you've worked out a solution of the mystery no one will care anything about it. You probably won't be in office. They're going to start circulating a recall petition against you tomorrow morning. Everyone in the city feels you either sold out or were made a fool of. The minute you let it be known you're trying to locate Shirley Arden, after having had that little dinner scene with her last night, and particularly when it becomes known that you can't find her, you're finished. It doesn't make any difference *how* many murder mysteries you solve.

"And don't ever underestimate this Carl Bittner. He's clever. He's a newspaper man who knows all of the angles. He knows how to use propaganda and sway public sentiment. While you're patiently solving this mystery step by step, Bittner will take some short-cut and you'll read the solution spread all over the front page of *The Blade*."

"All right," Selby said, grinning, "you win. We solve the murder by four-thirty."

"Four-fifteen," she said. "In fact, the solution has to be a little earlier so I can get the highlights of the story telephoned over to the office."

"When do we start?" he asked her, grinning.

"We start now."

"All right," he said, "here's something for you to consider. Here's the camera which the dead man had in his possession. For some reason or other, that camera seems to have a very peculiar significance. Someone tried to steal it from me in Hollywood last night."

"Because of the films which were in the camera?" she asked, her eyes showing her excitement.

"I wouldn't say so," he said. "The films in the camera show a very fine assortment of street scenes. In fact, they show the main streets of Madison City."

"But there may be something on them. There may be something significant we could catch, something which would show the purpose he had in coming here."

"There is," he told her grimly, "there's something very significant on them."

"What is it?"

"The new ornamental street lighting pole at the corner in front of the Madison Hotel. That pole was being put up Tuesday morning when I drove down to the hotel after the body had been discovered. In other words, the pictures in that camera were taken anywhere from hours to days *after* the man was killed."

"But how could that have happened?"

He shrugged his shoulders.

"The camera was in the suitcase when you went to the hotel?"

"Yes."

"Then the films must have been substituted."

"How?"

"What happened to the camera?"

"The coroner took it and kept it in his safe."

"But someone might have substituted films."

He laughed and told her, "That's pretty much of a job. It would take some time. You see, these films aren't the ordinary type of roll films. They're not backed with black paper and . . ."

He broke off suddenly, to stare moodily at her and said, "So that's it."

"What?" she asked.

"Rogue being poisoned."

"What about him?"

"That's the coroner's dog, a big police dog who watches the place. Someone poisoned him. The poison was cunningly concealed and placed in a half dozen different places."

"Oh, yes, I remember. I didn't know his name was Rogue."

"That was yesterday. Shortly after we came back from Riverbend."

"And the poisoning was successful?"

"I don't know whether the dog died or not, but he had to be removed to the veterinary hospital."

"Then that was done so someone could substitute the films."

Selby said, "If that's true, it was fast work, because I picked up the camera right afterwards."

"But the coroner was very much attached to his dog, wasn't he?"

"Yes."

"And he was down at the veterinary's trying to see whether the treatment would be successful?"

"Yes."

"Then that's it," she explained. "The films must have been substituted while he was down there. You can fix that time within very narrow limits. It probably won't be over half an hour altogether."

Selby nodded and said, "*That's* a thought. How does the sheriff stand on this thing?"

"You mean what are his reactions to the piece in *The Blade?*"

"Yes."

"I don't know," she said. "Of course, he has his own political future to think of."

"I'm just wondering," Selby said. "No . . . I'm not either. The mere fact that I think I'm wondering shows how warped my mental perspective is. Rex Brandon isn't the type who would throw me over. He'll stick."

As though he had taken his cue from the words, Sheriff Brandon opened the door of Selby's private office and said, "Hello, folks, I'm walking in unannounced."

His big black sombrero was tipped back on his head. A home-made cigarette dangled from a corner of his mouth. His face showed the lines of character emphasized as he twisted his mouth in a one-sided grin.

"Well, old son," he said, "it looks as though we've put our foot in it, doesn't it?"

Selby said, "Where do you get that 'we' stuff? I'm the one that's in bad. You're sitting pretty. Go ahead and watch your own political fences, Rex, don't get tied up with me. I'm a political leper."

The sheriff's face showed genuine surprise.

"Listen, son," he said, "you don't mean that."

"Sure I mean it. I'm in bad; you're not. There's no reason why you should suffer by my mistakes."

The sheriff sat down heavily on the chair. "I never expected to hear you talk that way," he said.

"What way?"

"Turning against a partner."

"You mean I'm turning against you," Selby demanded incredulously, "because I won't let you share in my disgrace?"

"Well, I wouldn't exactly put it that way," the sheriff

said, "but we're in this thing together and, somehow, it don't look right for you to . . . well, to figure there's any question about where I stand."

Sylvia Martin took down the telephone and said, "Get me the city editor of *The Clarion*. . . . Hello, this is Sylvia, change that headline to read, 'SELBY AND BRANDON SOLVE MURDER.' . . . Yes, I'm on the inside of the story now. It's all ready to break. They've got the real murderer all tied up. They're just perfecting their case now before they strike. The arrest will be about three-thirty or four o'clock this afternoon. We've got an exclusive on it. I'll have the story all ready so I can telephone it in. . . . No, I'm not going to give you the story now. . . . No, it isn't all a bluff. . . . Yes, I know I'm staking my job on it. . . . All right, good-by." She slammed the receiver back into place.

Selby looked at her moodily and said, "So *your* job hangs on it too, does it?"

"Sure," she said cheerfully.

Selby pulled the films from his pocket. "Well, Sheriff," he said, "here's about all I've done. I've got a beautiful assortment of photographs of the main streets of Madison City."

"Those were the films that were in the camera?"

"Yes. And those films were taken long after the man was dead."

"What?"

"It's a fact."

"We were discussing," Sylvia said, "how the films could have been switched in the camera. We've about decided that when the coroner's dog was poisoned, it was because someone wanted to switch films."

"What time was the dog poisoned?" Brandon asked.

"Well," Selby said, "we can soon find out about that."

He reached for the telephone, but it was ringing before his fingers touched it.

He picked up the receiver, said, "Hello," and heard Shirley Arden's penitent voice.

"Douglas Sel..." she asked, "I mean Mr. Selby?"

"Yes," he said, stiffening.

"I'm over at the hotel," she told him. "Strictly incognito. That same room—five fifteen."

"What kind of a run-around is this?" he demanded. "You certainly gave me enough of a double-cross last night. If you want to know the details, you can pick up a copy of *The Blade*."

"Yes," she said contritely, "I've already seen it. Please come over."

"When?"

"Right away."

"All right," Selby said grimly, "I'm coming. And I'm not going to be played for a sucker this time, either."

He slammed up the telephone.

Sylvia Martin was looking at him with wide, apprehensive eyes.

"Shirley Arden?" she asked.

He nodded.

"You're going, Doug?"

"Yes."

"Please don't."

"Why?"

"I don't know. I just don't trust her. She's clever. She's

an actress. She's ... got glamor and I'm afraid she's going to hypnotize you."

"She's not going to hypnotize me *this* time," Selby promised.

"Oh, please, Doug. You stay away. Have Sheriff Brandon serve a subpoena on her to appear before the grand jury. It's your one chance to show that you weren't bribed. This may be a trap, and, even if it isn't, suppose Bittner finds out about her being there and about you going over? Can't you see what we're fighting for? We're working against time and it means so much ... so much to *all* of us."

He shook his head doggedly and said, "I promised I was going, I'm going to go. I owe that much to my self-respect. She called me in confidence, and I'll see what she has to say before I betray that confidence."

"She's a little two-faced hypocrite," Sylvia said savagely. "Every time you've come in contact with her you've been strung along. The proof of the pudding is in the eating. You should have found *that* out by this time."

Selby said simply, "I'm sorry, Sylvia, but I'm going."

Her lip quivered. She glanced beseechingly at Rex Brandon.

The sheriff shook his head, sucked on his brown-paper cigarette and exhaled a thin wisp of pale blue smoke from the corner of his mouth.

"No use, sister," he said. "He's going."

Selby started for the door. He looked back, to see Sylvia Martin's pleading eyes, then he closed the door.

18

Doug Selby knocked at the door of five fifteen, then, without waiting for an answer, pushed the door open.

Shirley Arden was coming toward him. She was alone in the room.

He closed the door behind him, stood staring at her.

"Well?" he asked.

"I'm sorry."

"You should be."

"I am. I shouldn't have believed Ben. Ben is excitable and suspicious. But you know how it looked to him."

"I'm listening," Selby said.

She came close to him, put her hands on his shoulders. Eyes which had thrilled millions of picture fans stared into his with compelling power.

"Am I forgiven?" she asked.

"That depends," he told her.

"Depends on what?"

"Depends on what you say and how you say it."

211

"What do you want me to say?" she asked.... "Oh, please, please. I don't blame you for being angry with me, but after all it was such a shock, and Ben's explanation sounded so logical."

"That I'd done it as a publicity stunt?"

"Yes. And to drag me into it. He insisted that you were back of the leak to the newspapers. He warned me you'd string me along, but that you'd try to drag me into it so you could get the big news syndicates interested, focus a lot of publicity on yourself, and capitalize on it politically."

"Yes," he said bitingly, "you can see how much I've capitalized on it. Trying to play square with you is going to make me the laughingstock of the whole county."

She nodded and said contritely, "I realized that when I heard about *The Blade*. I came here because I couldn't go back on you. You'd been square and big and fine and genuine."

"I presume," he said, "Ben Trask sent you here and rehearsed you in what you were to say."

"Ben Trask thinks I'm on an airplane headed for Mexico City to recuperate."

"Trask was up here the day of the murder?" he asked.

She nodded.

"And the day before?"

Again she nodded.

"Do you suppose his interest in keeping things under cover is selfish?"

She shook her head.

"What's your hold on George Cushing?" he asked.

She said simply, "He's my father."

Selby's face showed his surprise. "Your what?" he asked.

"My father. He kicked me out to shift for myself when I was eleven. After I made fame and riches, he hunted me out."

"And how about this preacher?" he asked.

She motioned him to a chair.

"I'm going to tell you the truth," she said. "I don't care what happens. I don't care what my father or Ben Trask think."

"Go on," he told her.

"No one knows very much about my past," she said. "The fan magazines carry a synthetic story every once in a while about my having been raised in a convent, which is a lie. I was raised in the gutter."

He stared at her in steady, watchful scrutiny.

"When I was seventeen," she said, "I was sentenced to a reform school as an incorrigible. If I'd gone to the reform school, I'd have *been* incorrigible. But there was one man who had faith in me, one man who saw the reason for my waywardness."

"You mean Larrabie?" Selby asked.

"Yes. He was a minister who was taking a great interest in human welfare work. He interceded with the judge and managed to get me paroled for a year. He made me realize I should have some ambition, that I should try to do something for myself. At the time, I thought a lot of what he said was just the old hooey, but I was impressed enough by him and cared enough for him so I tried to make good. Four years later I was an extra in Hollywood. Those four years had been four years of fight. I'd never have stuck it out, if it hadn't been for his letters, for his steady, persistent faith, for the genuine, wholehearted goodness of the man."

"Go on," he told her.

"You know what happened after that. I played extra parts for a year. Then I had a minor speaking part. A director thought I showed promise and saw that I had a lead in a picture."

He nodded.

"Last week Larrabie telephoned me," she said. "He said he had to see me right away, that he couldn't come to Hollywood because of a matter which demanded his attention here. He told me he needed five thousand dollars— in fact, he told me that over the telephone.

"I went to the bank and drew out five thousand dollars in five one-thousand-dollar bills. I came up here. He had a scenario he wanted to sell. It was entitled *Lest Ye Be Judged.* You know how hopeless it was. I explained to him that I didn't have anything to do with the purchase of pictures. It was, of course, founded on my life story."

"Then what?"

"Then he told me what he wanted with the five thousand dollars. A very close friend of his, a man by the name of Brower, was in a financial jam. Larrabie had promised to get him the money. He'd been working for months on that scenario. He thought it was a masterpiece. He felt that with me to give it a good word he could easily sell it for five thousand dollars. I told him to forget the scenario and gave him the five thousand dollars. I told him to consider it as a loan."

"That was all?"

"That was all."

"Did he tell you why he was registered here under the name of Brower?"

"He said he was working on some business deal and the man for whom he was working told him the thing must be kept under cover. He said he'd written the man from Riverbend, and the man had telephoned him, told him that it would be dangerous to come here and register under his right name; that the thing to do was to come here without anyone knowing he was here and register under a fictitious name."

"Did he tell you any more about that?" Selby asked.

"He said the man asked him if he'd told anyone about having written. Larrabie said he hadn't. Then the man said that was fine and to come here without letting a soul know—not even his wife. Poor Larrabie thought it would be less wicked to register under the name of someone else than it would to use a purely fictitious name. So he took Brower's identity—borrowed his driving license and wallet. Brower was in hiding, afraid he'd be arrested for embezzling some church money or something. He was waiting in Los Angeles to hear from Larrabie."

"Larrabie said he'd written a letter to the man he was to meet here?"

"Yes."

"He didn't tell you who the man was?"

"No."

"Didn't give you any idea?"

"No."

"Look here," Selby told her, "every time I've talked

with you, you've purported to tell me the truth. Every time it's turned out to be something less than or radically different from the truth."

She nodded mutely.

"What assurance have I that you're telling me the truth this time?"

She came toward him.

"Can't you see?" she said. "Can't you see why I'm doing this? It's because you've been so splendid. So absolutely genuine. Because you've made me respect you. I'm doing this—for you."

Selby stared at her thoughtfully.

"Will you stay here," he asked, "until I tell you you can go?"

"Yes, I'll do anything you say—*anything!*"

"Who knows you're here?"

"No one."

"Where's Cushing?"

"I don't know. He's under cover. He's afraid the whole thing is going to come out."

"Why should he be so afraid?"

She faced his eyes unflinchingly and said, "If my real identity is ever known, my picture career would be ruined."

"Was it that bad?" he asked.

She said, "It was plenty bad. Very few people would understand. Looking back on it, I can't understand, myself. Larrabie always claimed it was because I had too much natural energy to ever knuckle down to routine."

"You staked Cushing to the money to buy this hotel?" Selby asked.

"Yes. And I keep this room. It's mine. It's never rented. I come and go as I want. I use it for a hideout when I want to rest."

"Did Larrabie know that—about your room here?"

"No. No one except my father and Ben Trask knew of this room."

"Then why did Larrabie meet you here?"

"I don't know. He caught a glimpse of me as I slipped into the room and, of course, knew me at once, and felt free to knock. He's been sort of a godfather to me."

"Did Larrabie know your father?"

"No. He'd never seen Dad—except that he may have met him as the owner of the hotel."

"But he must have known generally of your father?"

"Yes. He knew *about* Dad years ago ... things that weren't very nice."

"What's been Cushing's past?" Selby asked.

She shrugged her shoulders and said, "Pretty bad. I presume there was a lot to be said on his side, but it's one of those things people wouldn't understand. But, after all, he's my father, and he's going straight now. Can't you see what a spot I was in? I *had* to lie, had to do everything I could to throw you off the track. And now I'm sorry. I tried my best to give you a hint about the real identity of the body when I said that he was a 'Larry' somebody from a town that had the name 'River' in it. I figured you'd look through the map, find out the number of California towns that had 'River' in their names, and telephone in to see if a pastor was missing."

"Yes," he said slowly, "I could have done that, probably

would have, if I hadn't had another clew develop."

He started pacing the floor. She watched him with anxious eyes.

"You understand?" she asked.

"Yes."

"I *couldn't* have done any differently. You *do* see it from my standpoint, don't you?"

"Yes, I see it from your standpoint."

"But, you're acting . . . so sort of . . . Tell me, this isn't going to prevent us from being friends, is it? I admire and respect you. It's meant a lot to me, just having met you. You're sincere and genuine. There's no pose about you, no false front. I don't usually offer my friendship this way. . . . I need friends like you. I'm surrounded with the glitter and glamor of personalities that are as false as the fronts of the motion picture buildings on a set. . . . Do you understand?"

Selby stared steadily at her.

"Over there," he said, waving his arm in the general direction of the courthouse, "there's a girl waiting. She's had faith in me and what I stand for. She's staked her job on my ability to solve this mystery by four o'clock this afternoon, simply because she's a wholehearted, loyal friend. She hasn't any money, smart clothes, influential friends or fine houses.

"I don't know whether I can tell you this so you'll understand it, but I'll try. If I give you my friendship, I'll be running back and forth to Hollywood. I'll be impressed in spite of myself, by the artificial glitter you're complaining of. I'll gradually see the limitations of my friends here, limitations which aren't deficiencies of character, but of environment. I'll get so I unconsciously turn up my nose when I ride in rattling, dust-covered, cheap automobiles. I'll adopt a patronizing attitude toward the things of this county and assume an urban sophistication.

"You ask me to understand why you lied to me. I do understand. From your viewpoint there was nothing else you could have done. Damn it, I can almost see your viewpoint clearly enough so it seems the *logical* thing for you to have done.

"To hell with it. Your life lies in the glitter and the glamor. Mine lies with the four-square friendships I've made in a community where everyone knows everyone else so intimately there's no chance for a four-flusher to get by."

He strode toward the door.

"I like *you*," he said. "I don't like your environment. You hypnotize me. You always have, ever since I met you, but I'm not playing moth to the flame of your environment. I'm checking out."

He jerked the door open.

"Where are you going?" she asked, panic in her eyes.

"To solve that murder," he said, "and to keep faith with a girl who would no more lie to me than she'd cut off her right hand."

She stood staring at him, too proud to plead, too hurt to keep the tears from her eyes.

He stepped into the hallway, slowly closed the door behind him.

19

Selby pushed his way through the door of his private office to encounter the disapproving eyes of Sylvia Martin.

"Well?" she asked.

"She told me the truth, Sylvia," he said, "the whole truth."

"Again?" she inquired sarcastically.

Selby went on doggedly, "Now that I know all the facts, I can appreciate how impossible it was for her to have done any differently than she did. It would have utterly ruined her career."

"So," Sylvia said, "she decided to ruin yours instead. That's what I hate about her, Doug. . . . It's what she did to you—and what she's trying to . . . Oh, hell, skip it! . . . Now that you have her story, do you know who the murderer is?"

"I think I do."

"Brower?" she asked.

He didn't answer her directly but said, "Sylvia, I want you to check my conclusions. I'm going to go over this thing with you step by step. First, I'm going to tell you what Shirley Arden told me. I'm going to ask you, of course, to regard it as a sacred confidence."

He began at the beginning and told her everything the actress had told him. When he had finished, she said slowly, "Then, if that story is true, Brower had no reason to murder Larrabie."

Selby nodded.

"And Brower's silence is due to an attempt to protect himself against some misappropriation of cash."

Again Selby said, "Probably it wasn't a misappropriation. Larrabie wouldn't have helped him out of an embezzlement. The probabilities are Brower had the money in cash and the cash was stolen, or else some friend betrayed him.

"The really significant thing about the whole business is that, despite the importance of getting that five thousand dollars, Larrabie wouldn't leave Madison City. Now, then, Larrabie had written some man with whom he was to do business here. That man telephoned him, asked him particularly if anyone knew of the letter, and then asked Larrabie to come here and register under an assumed name, using the utmost secrecy."

"Well?" she asked.

"The man who got the letter wasn't the man to whom it was written," Selby said.

"What are you talking about, Doug? You can't know that."

"So far," he told her, "I am just indulging in theories. Now, let's start checking up on facts."

She glanced at her wristwatch and said ironically, "Yes, my editor always likes facts. Particularly when the paper is going to accuse someone of murder."

"The first thing to do," Selby said, "is to study those photographs again."

"Why?"

"To find out *just* when they were taken. Take a magnifying glass, Sylvia, and study every detail. See if you can find some definite time clew. While you're doing that I'll be doing some other stuff."

"What other stuff?" she asked.

"Detective chores," he told her, grinning.

He picked up the telephone and said, "Get me Sheriff Brandon." A moment later he said, "Rex, I've got a lot of news and a lot of theory. The news isn't worth a damn unless the theory checks with the facts, so I want to find out the facts.

"I'm going to give you the manufacturer's number on that miniature camera. I want you to find out what dealer had such a camera in stock. Trace it through the wholesaler and retailer, get a description of the purchaser."

He read off the numbers on the lens and body of the camera and then said, "Just as soon as you get that information, let me know. But get it and get it at once, at all cost. . . . And here's something else, Rex. It's a bet I'm afraid we've overlooked. Try to bring out any latent fingerprints on the space bar of that portable typewriter. Do it as soon as possible."

"Okay," the sheriff said. "In the meantime I'm trying to trace Cushing. I think I'll be able to put my finger on him inside of an hour."

Selby frowned, said slowly, "Well...Okay, but don't get rough with him. And be sure I can reach you by telephone. I may want some fast action. I'll explain later."

He hung up the telephone and called the coroner.

"Harry," he said, when he had the coroner on the line, "I want to know something about Larrabie's suitcase."

"All right, what about it?"

"You took it into your custody?"

"Yes."

"Kept it in your office."

"Yes, in the back room."

"And Rogue, your police dog, was always on the premises?"

"Yes."

"When was the dog poisoned?"

"Why, yesterday morning—you were there."

"No, no, I mean when did you first find out he'd been poisoned?"

"It was sometime around twelve o'clock. I'd been out and when I came back the dog seemed sick. He wagged his tail to show he was glad to see me, and then dropped down on the floor and drooped his ears. His eyes had a peculiar round look to them, I can't tell you just how they looked because you'd have to know the dog to appreciate his change of expression. Dogs' expressions change just like people's do."

"And where was the dog when you came back?"

"In my office; but there's a narrow door leading to the back yard, so he could get out, if he'd wanted to."

"But he was where he could guard the office."

"Sure. No one could possibly have entered that office. Rogue would have torn them to pieces."

"Thanks," Selby said. "I just wanted to make certain. I think the poisoning of the dog is *particularly* important."

"So do I," Perkins said. "If I can find out who did it, you'll have another homicide case on your hands."

"How's the dog getting along?" Selby asked.

"He's going to pull through all right. Dr. Perry sat up with him all night. It was touch and go for a while, but he's going to be okay."

Selby hung up the telephone as Amorette Standish entered the room, and said to Sylvia Martin, "Your city editor's been calling up. He says he has to have some basis for that story. He says that, so far, there hasn't been a darn thing except your unsupported statement to back up the story, while all the evidence he can get is pointing the other way."

Sylvia looked up from the strip of films, grinned and said, "Did he say 'not a *darn* thing,' Amorette?"

"No," Amorette said, smiling, "he didn't say '*darn* thing.' He was madder than a wet hen. He used plenty of language."

"You tell him I'm too busy to come to the telephone," Sylvia said, "that I'm working on the details of the yarn and getting the facts all co-ordinated; that the story's absolutely okay and he can count on it. Better throw a scare into him. Tell him a Los Angeles paper has offered me a thousand dollars for the inside yarn and is holding a wire open to the office. Ask him if he wants to be scooped on a local story by a Los Angeles newspaper."

Amorette sighed and said, "Well, I'll put cotton in my ears and try to put it across."

"It won't be so bad," Sylvia said cheerfully, "if you can stick it out for the first ten seconds, the copper wire will melt and short the connection, so you won't have to hear the rest of it."

She turned to Selby and said, "Doug, these pictures were taken Wednesday noon."

"How do you know?" he asked, his voice showing his excitement.

"You can analyze the shadows, for the time of day. They show the picture was taken right around noon. Now, then, the Rotary Club meets at the Madison Hotel every Wednesday. When it meets, there isn't enough room for the members to park their cars on the main street and in the parking lot next to the hotel, so they spread down the side street and take every available parking space. At other times during the day it is very seldom the parking spaces on the side street are filled up.

"Now notice this picture. It shows the main street. Now here's the next one, that's looking down the side street. You see, there isn't a single vacant parking space on the whole street. I'll bet anything you want, these pictures were taken Wednesday noon, while the Club was having its meeting."

Selby said slowly, "That's darned good reasoning, Sylvia. I think I'll have to put you on my staff."

"You sure will," she told him, "if we don't have some facts for my city editor pretty quick. I can stall him just about so long and then I'll be finished. At that time I'll be completely and entirely out of a job."

"Well," he told her, "you can't get on up here because I'll be out of a job, too."

He picked up the camera, studied it carefully and put it back in its worn leather case.

"Why is the camera so important?" Sylvia asked. "And how could those pictures have been taken so long after Larrabie's death?"

"That," he told her, "is the thing on which any real solution of this case must turn. It's a fact which doesn't coincide with any of the other facts. In other words, it's like an odd-shaped piece in a jig-saw puzzle, something which looks difficult but really furnishes the key to the whole business, if it's interpreted correctly."

He picked up the telephone, called Dr. Perry, and when he had him on the phone, said, "Doctor, this is Doug Selby, the district attorney. For reasons which I won't try to explain over the telephone, the poisoning of Perkins's dog becomes a clew of greatest importance. How's the dog coming along?"

"I'm going to pull him through," Dr. Perry said. "I worked with him most of the night. If I hadn't gotten him just when I did, it would have been too late. Even ten minutes longer would have been fatal."

"Can you tell me anything about the poison that was used?"

"I think," Dr. Perry said, "that the poison was compounded by an expert. In other words, the man who did it was either a doctor or a chemist, a druggist or someone who knew a great deal about drugs, and probably something about animals."

"I wonder if you can take time to run up to the office for a few minutes?" Selby asked. "I want to get some definite and detailed information. I'm expecting to bring this case to a head within the next couple of hours."

"You mean you're going to find out who put the poison there?"

"I think I'm going to go farther than that," Selby told him, "and find out who murdered Larrabie. But keep that under your hat. I'm telling you because I want you to realize how important your co-operation may be."

"I'm dropping everything and coming right up," Perry promised.

"Thanks," Selby told him.

He hung up the telephone, returned to a study of the strip of negatives, then he rang up the manager of the telephone company and said, "I'm particularly interested in tracing a call which was sent from Madison City some time within the last week or ten days to William Larrabie at Riverbend, California. I wish you'd look back through your records and see what you can find out about that call, and let me know."

Receiving a promise of assistance, Selby dropped the receiver back into place and turned to meet Sylvia Martin's anxious eyes.

"Doug," she pleaded, "is this all a bluff, or do you have a theory?"

"I've got a theory," he said.

"Well, for the love of Mike," she pleaded, "kick through. I'm in on this, too, you know. And, if things start breaking, I've got to know enough so I can keep the story straight."

He started pacing the floor, talking in the mechanical monotone of one who is thinking out loud. "A hotel," he said, "is a peculiar place. It furnishes a temporary home for hundreds of people. People are all very much alike. They have their jealousies, their loves, their hatreds, their hopes and ambitions. They practice their little deceptions. Their lives flow on in a regular routine rhythm, all being enacted within a few feet of each other.

"Here in this hotel, on the night of the murder, we had a minister of the Gospel in one room, a young couple who saw fit to register under assumed names in an adjoining room. And, somewhere in the background, was another minister who was in a serious financial predicament. He had to have money and have it at once. It was an amount which was far beyond what he could hope to obtain by any legitimate means. And in that hotel we had a room kept by a prominent motion picture actress. The hotel was operated by her father. No one knew of the relationship. No one knew of certain chapters in the life of this actress.

"We happen to know these things about these few people. There were others about whom we don't know, but who must have had their own family skeletons, their own fears and hopes. They were all sleeping under the one roof."

"Brower wasn't there," she pointed out.

"No one knows where Brower was," Selby said. "He might or might not have been there."

"But he was registered in Los Angeles."

Selby smiled and said, "If you are going to be technical about it, there wasn't any reason why Brower couldn't have registered in the hotel in Los Angeles, left Los Angeles, gone to the Madison Hotel and taken a room under another name."

Her face showed excitement. "Did he, Doug?" she said. "Did he? Oh, Doug, if we could *only* get something like that."

He smiled and said, "Not yet, Sylvia, I'm simply mentioning possibilities."

"But why point them out in just that way?"

"Because," he said, "I want you to understand one fundamental thought, because it is of particular importance in the solution of this case."

"What is it?" she asked. "I don't see what you are getting at."

"What I'm trying to establish is that people are, after all, very much alike. They have the same problems, the same complexities of life. Therefore, when we find what these problems and complexities are in the case of some of the people who were in the hotel, we shouldn't make the mistake of considering that those problems must be inter-related merely because the people were temporarily thrown together in a physical environment."

There was something ominous in her voice as she said, "Doug, are you starting out to try and prove that no matter what this actress did, she couldn't have been . . ."

Amorette Standish opened the door and said, "Dr. Perry's here, all out of breath. Says he broke every speed record in town and that you wanted to see him at once . . ."

"Yes," Selby said. "Show him in."

"Gee, Doug," Sylvia remarked, "I sure hope something comes of this. That outline you've just given me about the hotel and all of the people in it would make a swell build-up for a smashing newspaper story climaxing the murder mystery."

"Well," he told her, "we'll see if we can't..."

The door opened and Dr. Perry bustled into the room. He had quite evidently been hurrying, and was breathing through his mouth.

He grinned at Selby and said, "Those damn stairs... Not as young as I used to be... Out of condition."

"Sit down there," Selby told him, "and get your breath. I didn't mean for you to run yourself to death getting here, and you'll need some breath to answer questions. By the way, Amorette, I want to give you some instructions. And, Sylvia, you can help me, if you'll step this way for a moment. You'll pardon us for a minute, Doctor?"

"I'll say," Dr. Perry panted. "I could use a breathing spell very nicely."

Selby stepped into the outer room, drew Amorette Standish and Sylvia Martin close to him.

"Now listen," he said, "a call may come in about that camera. I'm anxious to find out..."

"Yes," Amorette interrupted, "Sheriff Brandon telephoned. He said not to disturb you, but to tell you he'd talked with Mrs. Larrabie. She told him the minister got the camera through a retailer who sent to a dealer in Sacramento for it. The sheriff has a call in for the retailer in Riverbend. And he's already talked with the wholesaler in Sacramento. They're looking for the number and are going to call back. The sheriff said both calls would come to this office. He left word for them to call you direct."

"All right," Selby said. "If the call comes in while I'm talking with Dr. Perry and you get the numbers, just come to the door and beckon to me. And, Sylvia, I think you'd better be where you can listen in on that telephone call, and be absolutely certain that the numbers are correct."

"But, when you already have the camera," Sylvia said, "why be so worried about the numbers?"

He grinned and said, "Perhaps I'm making assurance doubly sure."

She nodded dubiously. "And perhaps you're stalling around so I don't get a chance to hear what you tell Dr. Perry."

Selby laughed, stepped back into the private office, closed the door and said, "Doctor, you know something of the facts about Larrabie's death."

"I've read the papers. What about it?" Dr. Perry asked.

"It's my theory," Selby said, "that the man who arranged things so Larrabie took that dose of poison was a man who must have known something of medicine and who must not only have access to morphia but knew how to put it in a five grain tablet."

Dr. Perry nodded.

"Now, then, you say that the one who poisoned this dog showed a considerable knowledge of medicine. I want to know just what you mean by that?"

"I mean," Dr. Perry said, "that as nearly as I can find out, the poisoned meat contained not one active ingredient, but two. Moreover, the poisoning had been very skillfully compounded and had been placed in food combinations which would be particularly attractive to a dog."

"And that, coupled with the number of poison cakes which had been placed around, would indicate to you that the poisoner was *very* anxious to get the dog out of the way."

"Exceedingly so. He wasn't taking any chances. Any one of those poison cakes would have killed the dog."

"Now, in order to plant that poison on the inside of the room, the poisoner must have had access to that room, isn't that right?"

Dr. Perry's forehead twisted into a perplexed frown. "Why, of course," he said, "that goes without saying."

"Therefore the dog wouldn't have been poisoned merely so the poisoner could have had a few minutes in that room."

"Why?" Dr. Perry asked.

"Because he already must have had access to the room when he planted the poison."

"That's right. . . . But wait a minute—how *could* he have planted the poison with the dog there?"

Selby said, "That's exactly the point. You see, Doctor, we have more definite clews to work on when it comes to trapping the poisoner of the dog than we do in trapping the murderer of William Larrabie. Therefore, I want to be reasonably certain that one and the same man was guilty of both the dog poisoning and the murder. Then I want to concentrate on getting that dog poisoner."

"I see what you're getting at," Dr. Perry said slowly, "and I think I can assure you, Mr. Selby, both the dog poisoning and Larrabie's death had this much in common—they were the work of some man who knew something of drugs, who had an opportunity to compound a five grain tablet containing a lethal dose of morphia, or who had access to such a tablet. And such a tablet, of course, would be exceedingly rare in the normal course of medical use. Also, the man knew something about dogs."

Selby stared steadily at Dr. Perry. "Is there," he asked, "any chance that Harry Perkins might have poisoned his own dog?"

Dr. Perry's face showed startled surprise. Then he said swiftly, "Why, Mr. Perkins was all worked up about it. He was going to kill the man who did it. He told me to spare no expense. The man was actually crying when he thought the dog was going to die. There were real tears in his eyes."

"Nevertheless," Selby said, "he might have poisoned the dog and then rushed him to you in order to counteract the effects of the poison."

"But why would he have done that?"

"Because he would want to make it look like an outside job. Mind you, Doctor, I'm not accusing Perkins, I'm simply asking you a question."

Dr. Perry said, "You mean that unless the dog had been absent from the premises, which he wasn't, the person who dropped that poison inside of the room must have been someone the dog knew. A stranger might have tossed it over the fence, but a stranger couldn't have planted it in that room."

"That," Selby told him, "is right. Now, then, Perkins, I believe, is a registered pharmacist."

"I believe he is, yes."

"And the poison which was given the dog was rather quick acting?"

"Yes, very."

"Isn't it rather unusual that Perkins would have detected the symptoms of poisoning and brought the dog to you as soon as he did?"

"Well," Dr. Perry said slowly, "it depends, of course; some people know their dogs so well they can tell the minute anything goes wrong. Still . . ." he let his voice trail away into thoughtful silence.

At that moment Amorette Standish knocked on the door, opened it and beckoned to Selby.

"Excuse me for a moment," Selby said. . . . "Although, on second thought, Doctor, I guess that's everything I wanted to get from you. I'd like very much to have you make some investigation along the theory I've outlined and see if you can find out anything."

Dr. Perry clamped on his hat, strode purposefully toward the door.

"You can count on me," he said, "and also on my absolute discretion. I'll be at the coroner's for a few minutes, if you want to reach me. I have some questions to ask him.,"

"Thanks, Doctor," Selby said.

When Dr. Perry had left the office, the district attorney turned to Amorette Standish.

"We've got the numbers," she said in a low voice.

The door of the other office opened as Sylvia Martin came from the extension line. She nodded and said, "I have them here. The sale was made to Mr. Larrabie shortly before Christmas of last year."

"Well, let's check the numbers," Selby said.

He led the way to the private office, took the camera from the case, read out the numbers. Both girls nodded their heads. "That's right," they said.

At that moment the door of the outer office opened and Sheriff Brandon entered the room.

"Find any fingerprints on the space bar of the type-writer?" Selby asked.

"Yes, there are a couple of good ones we can use."

"Were they those of the dead man?"

"No."

"By the way," Selby said, "what number did I give you on that camera?"

The sheriff pulled a notebook from his pocket, read forth a string of figures.

Sylvia Martin exclaimed, "Why, those aren't the figures that *we* have, and . . . Why, they aren't the figures that are on the camera!"

Doug Selby grinned. "Rex," he said, "while I'm outlining a damn good story to Sylvia, would you mind sprinting down the courthouse steps? You'll find Dr. Perry just getting into his automobile. Arrest him for the murder of William Larrabie."

20

Sylvia Martin stared at Selby with wide open eyes. "You aren't bluffing, Doug?" she asked.

"No," he told her.

"Then give it to me," she said, looking at her wristwatch, "and hit the high-spots. I've got to get this story licked into shape. Give me the barest outline. Tell me how you doped it out, and tell me how you know Dr. Perry's guilty."

"Let's get back to what we know," he told her. "We know that Larrabie had business here. It was business other than raising the five thousand dollars."

"How do we know that wasn't his business?"

"Because he didn't leave here after he had the five thousand dollars in his possession."

"I see."

"We know that he wrote someone here in Madison City, that this someone telephoned him and made arrangements for him to come to Madison City with the utmost secrecy. That was the person with whom Larrabie was doing business, and it's reasonable to suppose that business was connected in some way with the Perry Estate, because Larrabie's brief case contained documents relating to two independent pieces of business; one was the Perry Estate and the other was the scenario.

"Remember, I warned you that all people had problems, that we mustn't make the mistake of feeling that all of these problems must be related merely because the people happened to be under the same hotel roof. As a matter of fact, the five thousand dollars, Brower's trouble, whatever it may have been, and Shirley Arden's relationship with Larrabie, were all entirely independent of the business which actually brought Larrabie here.

"We should have known that if we had stopped to think, because he came here instead of going to Hollywood. Any business with the actress would naturally have taken him to Hollywood, where he'd have supposed it would have been more convenient for her to have joined him, since he knew nothing of her connections here, and we know his business with her related to getting five thousand dollars, yet he stayed on here after that business had been completed.

"Now the man to whom Larrabie wrote his letter and with whom he had his business must have been friendly to Larrabie—that is, someone whom Larrabie was aiding. He'd hardly have followed instructions so implicitly from someone hostile to him."

"Go on," she said.

"There's a remarkable coincidence which has escaped everyone's attention," he said, "and probably furnishes the key to the entire situation, and that is that the *initials* of both claimants to the money in the Perry Estate are the same. Therefore, if Larrabie had written a letter addressed simply to 'H. F. Perry' at Madison City, that letter might have been delivered either to Herbert F. Perry, or to Dr. H. Franklin Perry. And, if the letter contained evidence relating to the marriage of the two decedents, and had fallen into the possession of Dr. Perry, naturally Dr. Perry would have realized his only hope to beat Herbert Perry's claim was to suppress this evidence. Now, remember that in the newspaper clippings which Larrabie had in his brief case, the claimant to the estate was described simply as 'H. F. Perry.'

"Of course, I can't *prove* right now that Dr. Perry telephoned Larrabie, found out that Larrabie hadn't let anyone know of the particular thing that he knew, therefore instructed Larrabie to come here and register under an assumed name; but I can surmise that.

"I can't *prove* Dr. Perry was closeted in conference with Larrabie, that he managed to give Larrabie a lethal dose of morphine either in a drink, in some article of food, or perhaps persuaded him to take a tablet as a cure for a headache, claiming it was merely aspirin; but I can surmise *that*."

"But you can't convict him on surmises," she pointed out, her eyes worried.

He grinned at her and said, "I can further surmise that there's one possibility in the Perry case the lawyers overlooked. While it's a matter of law that marriage has to be solemnized with certain formalities, it is also the law that where two people appear before a regularly ordained minister of the Gospel, state they have been living together, and ask to be married, the minister has authority under those circumstances to make a note of such marriage on the church records in order to make the marriage completely legal.

"If that happened, it would explain everything in the case. And, if Larrabie was a good photographer, which he was, he would have been very apt to have photographed that portion of the church records before leaving Riverbend. And, if Dr. Perry had killed him and then started thinking things over and read in the newspapers about the camera having been found in Larrabie's suitcase, he would have been certain to appreciate his danger in case those films were developed.

"So Dr. Perry decided he had to get possession of that camera. He had only one way of getting access to the place where Perkins kept the camera, and that was to poison the dog, because he knew Perkins would bring the dog to him for treatment; that then he would have a chance to go back to look the place over for poison. But he also knew he wouldn't have time to take the films *from* Larrabie's camera; but, if he played things right, he could switch cameras. So he purchased an identical camera and made plans for the substitution. In order to do that, he needed some exposed films in the camera, because he'd learned that some of the films in Larrabie's camera had been exposed.

"So he poisoned the dog and then, under the guise of looking for poison, returned to Perkins's place. Unfortunately for him, Perkins had called me and I was, therefore, present. But, offsetting that bit of particular bad fortune, he had the good fortune to find the camera where he could make a quick substitution. In order to do this, he needed to divert our attention. And he did this very successfully by dropping additional poison along the wall on the far side of the room. While we were all looking for poison, Perry had a chance to switch cameras. He thought, then, that he was in the clear, until he realized that I was going to check the numbers on the camera. Then he realized he needed to make a second switch. So I played into his hand by giving him a chance to come to my office and, when he had arrived, leaving him alone with the substituted camera. So far I can't *prove* anything. But, knowing the guilty person, I can start tracing telephone calls, looking on the church records at Riverbend for a record of that marriage. I think I can build up a pretty respectable case. And I can absolutely prove the substitution of those cameras, because he was the only one who had an opportunity to make this last switch, and I think the sheriff will find the camera we want in his possession.

"If we can reconstruct what must have happened, Perry lured Larrabie into a trap, insured keeping the facts exclusively within Larrabie's knowledge by impressing upon him the necessity for secrecy. He had an evening conference in Larrabie's room, gave the trusting minister a dose of morphia, probably claiming it was an aspirin. After the poison took effect, he calmly and methodically planted a box of sedatives and wrote the letter which he left in the typewriter which would make the death seem entirely natural. He'd previously opened the door of room three nineteen with a passkey, and he had only to barricade the door of three twenty-one, unbolt the connecting door to three nineteen, bolt it on the inside and leave through three nineteen, locking the door behind him. If I hadn't happened to notice the bolt wasn't in position on the minister's side of the door, the assumption would have been that no one could possibly have left the room. And that letter pointed to a natural death so cunningly that in the ordinary course of things the clews would have been pretty cold before an investigation was started.

"Perry overlooked just one thing, which was that when Larrabie registered under an assumed name, he hadn't taken a fictitious name, which Perry would naturally have expected, but had taken the name of an actual person.

"The little minister probably hated to be a party to any deception. Perry had instructed him to take a fictitious name. So Larrabie salved his conscience by borrowing the name of his colleague, Charles Brower, rather than taking a purely fictitious name. If the name *had* been purely fictitious, we'd have tried to notify a Mrs. Charles Brower at Millbank, Nevada, of her husband's death. Finding there was no such person, we'd have been baffled when it came to an identification of the corpse, but could reasonably have been expected to take the view death had been a natural one, induced by an overdose of sleeping medicine."

She studied him thoughtfully for a moment and said, "If that's right, you've done a perfectly swell piece of detective work. If it isn't right, we're both of us . . ."

She broke off as the door opened and Sheriff Brandon pushed Dr. Perry into the room.

"Get the camera?" Selby asked.

"Yes."

"Take his fingerprints," Selby said, "and check them with the fingerprints on the space-bar of that typewriter."

21

Madison City was shaken to its foundations as two news-papers made simultaneous appearance on the street. *The Blade* demanded the immediate recall of the district attorney on the ground of complete incompetence, upon the ground that he had been influenced by the monied inter-ests of Hollywood, that his head had been turned by the wiles of a clever actress, and that he had proven himself utterly unfit to discharge even the routine duties of his office.

The Clarion, in an "extra" which had evidently been printed and held in readiness to hit the streets at the same time as *The Blade,* carried great screaming headlines:

"SELBY AND BRANDON SOLVE MURDER MYSTERY!"

The newspaper carried complete details, even to a ver-batim copy of the marriage record of the Riverbend Meth-odist Church, as the contents of that record had been transmitted over long distance telephone at the request of the sheriff's office. It contained an interview with the fingerprint expert of the sheriff's office, stating there could be no doubt as to the identity of Dr. Perry's fingerprints, which appeared on the space-bar of the typewriter. And it contained a boxed-in paragraph giving a last minute flash announcing that Dr. Perry had confessed.

Sylvia Martin sat in the district attorney's office, reading the newspaper.

"A damned good story, Mr. District Attorney," she said, "even if we did write it."

He grinned across at her. "We had to save our jobs," he said.

"Say, Doug, know something?"

"What?"

"One of the big Los Angeles papers rang me up and offered me a swell job. Gee, Doug, the city editor was where he could hear my end of the conversation. He knew what it was. Gosh! but he was worried."

The district attorney's forehead showed furrows of concern. "Did you accept, Sylvia?"

"No," she said, "I told them I liked the local environment. . . . How about your Hollywood contacts, Doug? Going to play around with the movie crowd?"

"No," he told her, "I did the same thing you did."

"What's that?"

"Told them I liked the local environment."

She looked at him, gave a quick intake of breath.

"Really, Doug?"

"Really."

"Did . . . did you mean what I meant?" she asked.

"The question," he told her, "is: Did you mean what I meant?"

This Franklin Library edition of

THE D.A. CALLS IT MURDER

is set in Granjon,

a roman typeface bearing the name of the sixteenth-century

French type-founder Robert Granjon.

The display face, Aurora Grotesk, was selected by

designer Kate Nichols to complement this face.

Pat Butler designed the cover panel.

The frontispiece by David Tamura was specially commissioned

for this edition.

The acid-free paper is 70-pound Franklin Library Vellum White Offset,

made to archival standards by the P. H. Glatfelter Paper Company

of Spring Grove, Pennsylvania, for The Franklin Library.

The book was printed by R. R. Donnelley & Sons Co.,

Chicago, Illinois.

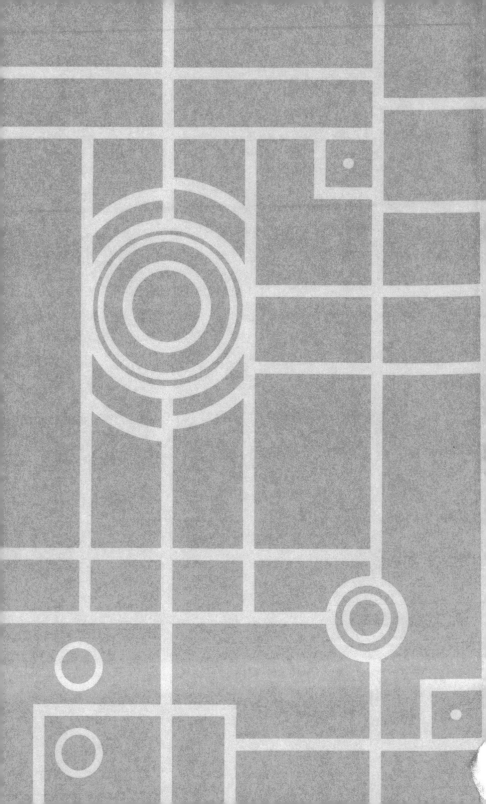